Dream Sister

Alexandra Whitaker

A Yearling Book

Published by
Dell Publishing
a division of
Bantam Doubleday Dell Publishing Group, Inc.
666 Fifth Avenue
New York, New York 10103

For Thomasin
My Beloved Younger Sister

ISBN: 0-440-40156-9

Reprinted by arrangement with Houghton Mifflin Company

Printed in the United States of America

April 1989

10 9 8 7 6 5 4 3 2

CW

Contents

1. A Humble Garret   1
2. Something Different   15
3. Direction North-Northeast   27
4. A Month of Sundays   38
5. Lily   47
6. A Miraculous Recovery   57
7. The Reading   69
8. On the Job   84
9. Ann Entertains   97
10. Exiled   110
11. Fun on the Farm   133
12. Dream Sister   148

CHAPTER ONE

A Humble Garret

Ann was ready to do battle.

What she had suspected for almost a year had today become a certainty: Ann needed a bedroom of her own. Until now she had shared one with her younger sister, Isabelle, but since her tenth birthday several weeks earlier she had felt there was something in that substantial two-digit number, 10, that required independence. How could a person of ten be expected to share a room with a five-year-old? It was ridiculous.

But would Mother agree? All day long in school, Ann had been trying to anticipate her mother's objections and to plan convincing responses. Now, as she ran up the steps to her house, she cleared her throat and rehearsed her speech one more time.

"Mother, I have something to tell you. I am afraid I simply cannot share a room with Isabelle anymore. I am ten years old now, and I need privacy. My studies are also suffering." (Ah, that's a good touch, she thought.) "It's hard to concentrate on my homework with Isabelle in the room because, as you know, she is a very loud and messy girl. I realize that this change may seem very sudden to you, but I think that if you consider carefully, you will agree that it must be."

It was a good speech: calm and direct. To counter any of her mother's possible protests, Ann would have to think on her feet, but her mind was clear and limber for the task ahead.

Mother was in her study, tapping away busily at the typewriter. Ann didn't usually disturb her when she was working, but today's mission was of special importance. Mother glanced up as Ann entered.

"Hello, darling. How was school?"

"Terrible," Ann growled, slinging her bookbag into the corner and dropping her jacket on the floor. She perched herself on the edge of the rocking chair and drew a deep breath. It was time to be firm.

"Mother," she began, "I have something to tell you. I'm afraid I simply cannot share a room with Isabelle anymore. I am —"

"Of course, sweetheart," Mother interrupted. "After all, you are ten now, and it's only natural for you to want a little privacy. It would probably be easier for you to get your homework done without Isabelle distracting you, too. Would you like the little room in the attic?"

"Uh . . . well, ah . . . yes." Ann was taken aback by how quickly her mother had accepted the idea.

"Then why don't you run upstairs and move your things before Isabelle gets home from Hilary's?" Mother smiled and returned to her typing.

A faint scowl of annoyance wrinkled Ann's brow as she went up the stairs, her unneeded arguments still spinning around in her head. The victory had been easy enough, but had it been . . . satisfying?

One look around what was henceforth Isabelle's room convinced Ann that, satisfying or not, the change was certainly for the better. As usual, the room was in total disorder. Isabelle's toys covered both beds and most of the floor, her clothes were scattered everywhere, and her sheets were hung like sails from the curtain rod to the bedpost, a sign that she had been playing pirates again. Last year Ann had tried putting a line of masking tape down the center of the room in an attempt to confine Isabelle's clutter to her own side, but it hadn't worked because the hall door was in Ann's half of the room. Isabelle was obliged to walk across Ann's half every time she went in or out, and wherever Isabelle passed, she left a trail of mess in her wake. Worse yet, Isabelle seemed to find asking permission to cross to the door fun, and she made up endless excuses for having to go in and out every two minutes. When she began asking permission for her dollies to cross too, Ann gave up. It was hopeless. But at last the problem was over.

Ann spent the next hour throwing her clothes and toys into cardboard boxes and lugging them up the narrow staircase to the attic. As she filled the last carton, she heard the thundering of her sister's footsteps on the stairs. This ought to be good, she thought.

Isabelle burst into the room, her long golden curls, her plump rosy cheeks, her enormous blue eyes, all glowing with energy and happiness.

Disgusting child, thought Ann.

Isabelle had other irritating habits besides her sloppiness and annoyingly constant good cheer. She borrowed Ann's things without permission, and she always asked Ann for help with everything. When Ann complained to her parents, they said that Ann must be patient for a while because Isabelle was younger. But Isabelle would *always* be younger!

"Hi, Annie!" Isabelle shouted. Isabelle nearly always shouted.

Ann busied herself with her packing and did not answer.

"What are you doing?" Isabelle asked.

"I'm moving out," Ann said. That sounded good.

"Where are you going?"

"From now on, I'm going to sleep in the attic room. I'm sick of sharing a room with you. You are loud and messy and babyish."

Isabelle's eyes were troubled.

"You mean I'll be down here all by myself?" she asked slowly.

"Yes, all by yourself," Ann answered. Then she cruelly added, "All by yourself . . . all night long."

There was a short silence, then suddenly Isabelle burst into laughter. "Goody, oh goody!" she shouted. "Now I have my own room!" She did a little dance on the rug and bolted down the stairs, screaming the good news to Mother.

What's the use of insisting on your rights and making a bold new change if nobody minds? Ann wondered. She hurled a book into the last box and dragged it up the stairs, barking her shin painfully on the top step.

The attic room was small and simply decorated. The ceiling sloped up on two sides, coming to a point in the middle, rather like a tent. On the far wall was a large dormer window that looked out over the back garden and brick row houses across the alley. The only furnishings were a desk and chair, a wardrobe, and a black iron bed. In one corner stood a small sink with a mirror over it. Ann had always liked this room, and she was especially charmed by the sink. It seemed the very height of independence to have a separate place in which to brush one's teeth. Ann hung up her dresses neatly on one side of the wardrobe and carefully arranged her toys and other clothes on the shelves on the other side. Lulled by this pleasant and orderly work, her grumpiness had begun to melt away when, in the bottom of the third box, she found THE PILE. Her dark mood descended upon her more heavily than ever. THE PILE! Would it haunt her forever?

The spring of the year before, Ann was nearly nine years old and finishing the third grade. She was doing very well in school; too well, in fact. Only halfway through the year, she had already worked her way to the end of the math and spelling books, far ahead of the rest of the class, and she grew bored. There was some talk of her going to a private school that was more challenging, but her parents' social and political views were against her leaving the public school system. At the end of the year, her teacher gave her a special test and arranged a meeting with Ann and her parents. It was decided that she should go directly from the third to the fifth grade.

"We're very proud of you, sweetheart," her mother told her. "You're a very smart little girl, and we're sure you'll do something wonderful one day."

"You're your mother's daughter, all right," Father added with an affectionate smile and a hug.

Ann's teacher laughed and said, "When you're famous, I'll be able to say that I knew you when you were only eight years old."

Famous? Ann thought to herself. I have to be famous? That sounds very hard.

That summer Ann began reading about the lives of famous people, and she became more and more depressed. It seemed that being smart was not enough. To be great, one had to be dedicated. One had to work all day and most of the night. What's more, all these important people had a head start on her! They were composing symphonies before they knew how to walk or designing cathedrals at the age of three. Ann would close those books gently and stare miserably ahead. "Here I am, nine years old already, and I've accomplished nothing. Nothing!"

Ann's own mother was a little like the successful people Ann read about. She was a rather famous writer of novels, short stories, and plays. Her first book, a collection of poems, had been published when she was only thirteen, and it included some poems she had written even before that! My mother didn't waste any time, Ann thought grimly. She was already hard at work when she was my age.

Determined to make something of herself before it was too late, Ann took her paintbox outside and painted a picture of a tree. She muttered to herself as she worked, tongue between her teeth, her attention focused rigidly on the task before her.

Ann, the famous artist, began painting at an early age. She surprised the whole neighborhood with the beautiful pictures of her tree period, working tirelessly to perfect her craft, painting day and night . . .

Ann became so carried away with the idea that she decided she absolutely must become a painter. She made up her mind to paint five pictures a day for the next five years, for she knew from her reading that success came only with constant practice. That day she enthusiastically dashed off five paintings. The next day she felt a little lazy, but she got her five done, hurrying through the last two. The third day Ann sat by the river, brush in hand, longing to go roller skating. After the second picture, she threw her paints into her bookbag and promised herself she would catch up the next day by doing eight.

The morning Ann's painting career came to an

end, she had put off so much work that in order to get back on schedule she would have had to paint twenty-four pictures before sunset. Twenty-four! Ann had been so filled with dread that she could hardly make herself get out of bed. Then, with a shriek of revolt, she had grabbed the paintbox and flung it into the darkest corner of her closet. That paintbox was the beginning of THE PILE.

Ann started many such projects, adventures into fields in which she might become a famous person. She began a journal, vowing to write in it every day, and when she found herself two weeks behind, the journal joined the paintbox. By the time she was ten, THE PILE contained the paintbox, the journal, a flute, ballet slippers, a partly embroidered sheet (she had intended to make her mother a tablecloth), a box of homemade Italian flash cards filled with words beginning with A (she had copied them from a dictionary, meaning to memorize the whole thing), a fishing rod, and a box of nails and a hammer left over from her most recent plan: to build a set of dining room furniture. THE PILE was something Ann preferred not to think about. She sometimes wondered if she had not already tried and failed at every possible profession. The chances are, she told herself glumly, I'll have to become a school cook, which was her idea of the lowest form of employment.

Now, as she sat in her new room and frowned at THE PILE, lurking reproachfully in the last box, Ann was struck by a wonderful and daring idea. Why not just throw it all away? But, no, she decided, I must keep it as a constant reminder of my laziness and failures. In the end she compromised and, in one bold gesture, tossed the box into the bottom of the wardrobe and slammed the door.

Then Ann came across her old teddy bear, Pecony. Poor Pecony, she thought, I haven't played with you for a long time. It is true that girls who are especially intelligent and destined for greatness don't have much time for their bears. It's one of the things they have to sacrifice for their careers. As she set Pecony on her desk so he could watch her work, she reflected bitterly: On top of everything else, I've failed as a mother. How does *my* mother manage to get everything done? She takes care of her children and cooks good meals and trims the shrubs and writes those long books. I guess some people are just born clever and hardworking, but that doesn't necessarily mean that their children will be. What if somebody writes a book about my mother's life?

  . . . *but despite her many literary triumphs, her life*

was not without cruel disappointment. Until her dying day one secret grief, one burning sorrow, tormented her: her older daughter, Ann, was a total dud.

Continuing to tidy up her room, Ann became deeply involved in a game. She narrated the story to herself as she worked.

. . . and so it was that little Ann was obliged to give up her comfortable room downstairs and to move into a humble maid's garret so her sister could have a room to herself. Her new stepmother had warned her that many things were going to change now that she was in charge, and many had. Little Ann did not mind, however, because she was a naturally sweet-natured child. Her sister, Isabelle, was the preferred daughter, and she always wore rich robes spun of gold and costly gems, but little Ann did not envy her finery any more than she envied her golden locks and baby blue eyes. Instead, she cheerfully arranged her few poor possessions in the stark garret that had no heat —

Here Ann glanced nervously around the room and was relieved to see a radiator next to the window.

— and she shivered as she cheerfully pulled her thin wrap around her and —

"Ann? Ann?" Mother called from downstairs. "It's time for dinner."

Ann was annoyed at the interruption, but she reasoned that she could continue the game during dinner. To set a better mood, she changed into an ugly orange dress she hated and went humbly down to the kitchen.

"May I help you, Mother?" she asked in a meek voice.

Little Ann had to wait on the rest of the family before nibbling her dry crust in the corner, but she didn't mind so long as —

"Why certainly, darling. That's very thoughtful of you." Mother laughed, hugging her.

Ann stiffened under the inappropriate hug and carried a bowl of peas out to the table. Her father and sister were already seated.

"Good evening, Father," Ann said softly.

Little Ann knew enough to be always respectful before her temperamental father, who often —

"Hello, honey," Father said, kissing her. "You look very lovely tonight."

They're ruining the game! Ann thought.

"Annie's wearing a dress!" Isabelle shouted. "Annie, why are you wearing that? You look funny!"

Oh, be quiet, Ann thought furiously, but then she realized that for once in her life, Isabelle was doing exactly the right thing.

. . . The beautiful Isabelle mocked Ann's poorhouse, hand-me-down clothing.

"Hush, Isabelle," Mother said, sitting down. "I think she looks very pretty. Ann, I'm glad to see you wearing that dress. I was afraid you didn't like it."

"Oh, by the way," Father said suddenly, "has anyone seen my hammer? I've been looking for it for months now."

Ann tensed guiltily. Yes, she'd seen it, but how could she say so without having to explain that embarrassing failure to surprise everyone by building a set of dining room furniture? She studied her plate and decided to say nothing.

Little Ann's father often baited her by accusing her of stealing his tools.

The rest of the meal passed satisfactorily. While the others talked and joked, Ann was careful not to join in the conversation, although she occasionally smiled a shy, frightened smile. And she did not take second helpings. Afterward, she carried all the dishes back into the kitchen. She even began to scrub the stove, but it was hot and tiring work, so she threw the sponge back into the sink.

Although little Ann wanted desperately to clean the stove as a gesture of humility and love, her stepmother would not let her for fear the clumsy girl would break it.

Ann raced up the two flights of stairs to her room and got ready for bed. She considered her face in the mirror while she brushed her teeth. She had a pointed face, large dark eyes, and straight dark hair cut shoulder length with longish bangs. I'm not beautiful, she thought. Not as pretty as Isabelle. But I'm pretty enough. At least I'm not as ugly as that pig, Patty Dorval. What would I do if I were Patty Dorval? Drink poison, probably. And with that Ann flung herself cheerfully on the squeaky iron bed and settled in to read a book of fairy tales before she fell asleep.

Late that night Ann had a strange and vivid dream. She dreamt she woke up suddenly because she had heard someone speak very nearby in a high, clear voice, like the tinkle of crystal. But she couldn't make out the words. Then she felt a cool, damp breeze on her face and heard a rustling sound. Looking around the room, she saw that the long white curtains of the dormer window were billowing in the wind. In her dream, Ann walked over to the window and stood in front of it for a minute, letting the gusts of night air lift her hair from her shoulders and blow her nightgown against her legs. Then she reached out to close the window, but her fingers met the smooth surface of the glass. How could that be? Puzzled, she lingered a moment longer, the wind in her face, her palms pressed flat against the windowpane.

Then she woke up, confused and sleepy in her bed.

CHAPTER TWO

Something Different

After glancing around the schoolroom and seeing to her satisfaction that she was the first one finished, Ann arranged her colored pencils with care on the top of her desk. Mrs. Weed had handed out fresh, blank maps of Africa, and the students were to fill in the countries, rivers, and mountain ranges. Although Mrs. Weed hadn't asked the students to color their maps, Ann liked to give hers that finishing touch. Her rivers were blue, her mountains brown, and her borders between countries neat black lines. She began to sketch a small giraffe in Kenya but decided that might be excessive and show-offish, so she erased it quickly before Mrs. Weed collected the papers and left the room. Ann sighed with pleasure. She really enjoyed school when everyone was neat, quiet, and busy.

Mrs. Weed was Ann's favorite teacher, and Ann suspected that she was Mrs. Weed's favorite student. It wasn't that Mrs. Weed chose Ann to erase the blackboard or run errands, for she was too good a teacher to show such favoritism, but she had a way of smiling at Ann that seemed to say "I know you know the answer, but before I call on you, I want to see if anyone else can get it." At the beginning of the year, when Ann had arrived fresh from the third grade, Mrs. Weed had gone to special trouble to make her feel at ease in her new class. Together they had raced through the fourth grade math book, and in a few weeks Ann had caught up with the other fifth-graders. Mrs. Weed was everything a teacher should be, and Ann promised herself that when she grew up and became famous, she would find Mrs. Weed and thank her for being efficient, intelligent, and kind.

Suddenly, however, the smile of contentment on Ann's face faded. Miss Delray had just burst into the room. Miss Delray was the reading teacher and anything but efficient, intelligent, and kind. Ann had been wary of her since the first day of school, when Miss Delray had given a speech that started with: "Now, people, I'm going to be frank with you, and I want you to be frank with me." That was a certain sign of a modern teacher, and Ann hated modern teachers with their messy, noisy classes in which no one could spell but everyone was devoted to "self-expression." Miss

Delray spent much more time talking about "personal involvement" and "discovering oneself" than about grammar and making logical sense.

"People?" Miss Delray began in her loud, singsong voice.

The schoolroom had become noisy. The departure of Mrs. Weed and the entrance of Miss Delray was always the signal to misbehave.

"People? I'm counting! One, two, three, four . . ."

It was one of Miss Delray's delusions that if she counted long enough the class would stop talking, out of respect, perhaps, or out of pity for her. Ann had often wondered where Miss Delray had gotten this stupid theory. One eventful afternoon she had reached thirty-eight before finally screaming, "All right!" Today she was not so patient. At "fourteen" she let out a mighty yell and a hush gradually fell over the room.

"Today, people, we are going to do . . . something different," she announced, her voice full of hopeful promise.

Ann rested her forehead on her hand in a gesture of despair. "Something different" was almost always something stupid. It usually meant that Miss Delray had thought of a way for them to "have fun" and "learn" at the same time.

"Patty, pass these around. One to each person," Miss Delray said. It made perfect sense to

Ann that Miss Delray's favorite was that revolting Patty Dorval. Smirking importantly as she went around the room handing out papers, Patty passed Ann without giving her one. It wasn't the first time this sort of thing had happened, and Ann wasn't going to stand for it.

"Miss Delray," she said in a loud, clear voice, "Patty didn't give me a sheet."

"Oh," Patty said, her piggy eyes bulging with mock surprise, "I forgot about Ann. It's easy to do because she's so tiny and quiet."

The class snickered at Patty's remark and turned to look at Ann. She was used to this. They had resented the arrival of a mere nine-year-old in their midst, and Patty was especially put out because Ann had replaced her as the best student. Ann snatched the paper from Patty's plump hand and glared angrily around the room. She saw one face, however, that gave her a friendly smile. That was Fernando.

Ann liked Fernando. He was quiet, good-looking, and the fastest runner in the fifth grade. And, like Ann, he was treated as an outsider by the class. Sometimes they teased him because he spoke with a slight accent, but Ann found his accent charming. She and Fernando used to walk to school together until one day Suzy Sprager, Patty's best friend, saw them together and shouted, "Ann loves Fernando! Ann loves Fernando!" It had been too much to bear, and Ann still blushed to think of it. The rumor had died down eventually, but Ann had avoided Fernando since then. She thought he understood why, and now she smiled back at him gratefully.

"People," Miss Delray said, "I want you all to look carefully at the papers I gave you."

The students looked and found that they were absolutely blank on both sides.

"There's nothing on them," Patty Dorval observed.

Miss Delray's face grew pink with excitement. "Exactly!" she pronounced triumphantly. "And do you know why that is?" She looked around eagerly, nearly bursting with the suspense of it all.

Ann's eyelids drooped. No, she didn't know, but she was sure the reason would be dumb.

"Why?" asked Suzy Sprager, breathless with anticipation.

Miss Delray struggled to contain her delight and to speak calmly. "I have just given you the script to a play we are going to perform right here and right now! It is blank — can you guess why? — because it's up to all of *you* to decide what characters you want to play, what lines you want to say, and what the story will be. I'm not going to have a *thing* to do with it. *It's all up to you!*" Miss Delray folded her arms emphatically and leaned back against the wall to demonstrate just how little she was going to interfere with their creative processes.

Amid the general babble of enthusiasm from the class, Ann sat stunned. In her wildest dreams she could not have imagined an assignment this stupid. In what way, she wondered dully, is a play with no characters or lines a play?

All around her, people jumped up and shouted out the roles they wanted.

"I'm a policeman," yelled Mike Dunk. "Hands up or I'll shoot!"

"I'm a poor crippled girl," Beth whined. "I have no mommy or daddy and nobody loves me. Who will take care of me?"

Ann shuddered and turned away.

"Miss Delray, may we move the desks?" asked Patty Dorval.

"Certainly!" Miss Delray was so eager to allow this freedom that she almost choked trying to get the word out. "Use your space, people. *Use your space!*"

Utter chaos broke out in the classroom. Chairs and tables were shoved against the walls. Pens and notebooks flew onto the floor. Ann's classmates charged to and fro, screaming at the top of their lungs. Jimmy crawled on the floor, biting people. He was a rabid dog. Patty Dorval was a fairy princess who twinkled about on her toes asking, "Where are my magic elves? Will you be my magic elf?" Others were fire engines, ballerinas, mayors, and elephants. Fernando stood, silent and motionless, in one corner. When asked what he was, he answered simply, "A street light."

Ann remained seated at her desk, ashamed to be a part of the scene. Every few seconds someone bumped into her, and she held on grimly to the bottom of her chair to keep from being knocked out of it. Suddenly she felt a moist hand on her shoulder and turned to find Miss Delray's broad face one inch from her own.

"And who are *you*, Ann?" Miss Delray asked in a syrupy voice.

"I'm a girl in school," Ann said through clenched teeth.

"Oh, Ann," Miss Delray said sadly, "I'd have thought you'd have more imagination than that. After all, with a mother like yours . . ."

Inwardly, Ann raged at the injustice of her teacher's remark. Would this day never end?

Ann's bookbag hit the living room wall a little harder than usual that afternoon. In the kitchen, she found Isabelle with two of her friends, Kate and Hilary, busily painting and eating cookies. Some of the cookies were slowly dissolving in a shallow pool of green paint water on the table-top.

"Annie, do you want to help me paint?" Isabelle asked. "Look, I'm making a bird in a tree with a —"

"You're making a mess," Ann said curtly. She took some salami and mustard out of the refrigerator. Why did Isabelle always clutter up the house with her idiotic friends? Didn't she see enough of them in school?

"Do you want a cookie?" Hilary held out a chocolate chip cookie smeared with purple paint.

"No. It's revolting," Ann said, and she carried her sandwich into the dining room. Mother was watering some plants on the windowsill and plucking off dead leaves.

"Ann," she said reproachfully, "you shouldn't be uncivil to Isabelle and her friends."

"They are loud, messy pigs," Ann explained.

"They are sweet little girls," Mother said firmly. "I often wish you would have some friends over. Aren't there any girls in school you'd like to invite? You could have tea and drink it by yourselves in the living room if you'd like."

Ann listened sulkily. She did not like to be reminded that she had no friends. Was it necessary to make such an issue of it? Ann just wasn't the type who could make friends, at least not in the fifth-grade class run by Patty Dorval. She had come close with Fernando, but that had ended in disaster. She didn't like anyone else in her class, and they certainly didn't like her.

Ann led a curiously solitary and friendless life. Her painting, dancing, and carpentry left her no time for idle chatting and frivolous tea parties, and she had no taste for purple cookies.

"If I liked stupid girls, I could invite over a whole houseful," Ann said with dignity.

Mother smiled at her a little sadly and patted her hair.

After supper that evening, Ann heard Isabelle singing to herself out on the front steps.

"My name is Is-a-belle. Is-a-belle. Is-a-belle. And my name is pret-ty."

Ann had always been rather jealous of her sister's name, finding her own a bit too plain, even if it had been borne by women in her family since colonial days. She went outside and sat down next to Isabelle, her elbows on her knees and her cheeks in her palms.

"Hi, Annie!" Isabelle shouted. Then she continued her little, tuneless song, "My name is Is-a-belle . . ."

"Your name wasn't always Isabelle," Ann said casually.

Isabelle laughed. "Oh yes it was."

"No," Ann said seriously. "You see, before you were born my name was Annabelle."

Isabelle looked confused. She always felt uncomfortable when she heard about that mysterious time before she was born.

"And when you were born," Ann continued, "your name was just Is."

"*Is?*" Isabelle asked doubtfully, trying out the odd sound.

"Is," Ann repeated, letting it sink in.

"But . . . that isn't pretty."

"No," Ann agreed. "In fact, it's very ugly. Mother and Father were worried because it was so ugly, so I told them that you could have my 'abelle.' Ever since then, your name has been Isabelle and mine just Ann."

For a long time Isabelle was silent. "Oh," she said softly, considering the enormity of her debt to Ann. "That was *very* nice of you, Annie."

Ann sighed. "Yes, I know. Sometimes I regret it a little, but then . . ." She looked at Isabelle with a frown. "But don't you ever tell Mother and Father I told you about this. They didn't want you to know so you wouldn't feel bad and greedy about taking my name."

"I'll never tell," Isabelle promised. "Thank you, Ann."

"That's all right," Ann said graciously, and she went up to her new room.

It was the blackest part of night when Ann's strange dream returned. She dreamt that a clear, tinkling voice had awakened her, and this time she could hear the words still echoing in her head.

"Don't you recognize me?" The voice sounded sad and disappointed.

Suddenly Ann remembered that she had had this dream the night before, too. She glanced around to see who had spoken, but the room was empty. The same cool, damp breeze wafted in from the window, a little more forcefully this time, ruffling the sheets on the bed. Timidly, Ann slipped out of bed and crept to the window. She knew even before she touched the glass that it would be closed. But when she looked out, she saw with surprise that the back yard, the alley, and the neighboring houses had disappeared. In their place was a brightly lit carnival ground. Very faintly she heard sounds of laughter and music. Then she saw a small figure wrapped in shawls, silhouetted by the colored lights of the merry-go-round. It seemed to be beckoning to her. Over the sounds of the fair the voice reached her again.

"Ann, don't you recognize me?"

Ann pressed her forehead against the cold

windowpane and stared down, her hair whipping wildly in the wind and slashing her cheek. She was overwhelmed with a strange feeling of sadness and urgency.

"I . . . I can't," she stammered. Then she awoke to find herself standing at the window. She leapt back into bed and buried herself under the comforting blankets.

CHAPTER THREE

Direction North-Northeast

As she walked to school the next day, Ann felt apprehensive and bewildered. She had never had a recurring dream before, and she didn't know what to make of it. Also, this dream was as vivid and clear as things she remembered, not hazy and vague like other things she had dreamt. The voice of the girl wrapped in shawls, the cool, moist wind somehow blowing through the closed window, the eerie lights of the carnival . . . it had all seemed so real. The little girl had been so disappointed that Ann failed to recognize her. Ann felt strangely guilty for not knowing who she was and confused about feeling guilty.

She was certainly in no mood to spend a long, dull day in school. She had considered pretending to be sick that morning so that she could stay home, but the idea of spending the whole day in her attic room was not inviting either. Resigned, she kept walking and, turning a corner, she caught sight of Fernando a little way in front of her. Quickly, she glanced up and down the street to make sure Suzy Sprager was not around.

"Fernando, wait," she called. Fernando turned around and smiled as she ran to catch up with him.

"Hi, Ann," he said. "We'd better hurry or we'll be late."

They had not walked far before Ann suddenly stopped short. "Fernando," she said, her voice tense with the wild idea she had just had, "let's . . . let's not go to school today. I don't want to. Do you? We aren't going to do anything important today, anyway. Just that stupid play, probably."

Fernando frowned uncertainly for a moment, then smiled. "Okay, Ann. But what do you want to do instead?"

Ann faltered. She had never skipped school before, and the idea seemed both exciting and frightening. She wondered if she should reconsider. Then she imagined what the day would be like if she did go: bossy Patty, pudgy Suzy, that oaf Mike Dunk, Miss Delray and her counting, more "self-expression" . . . No. School was definitely out of the question.

"Oh, I don't know," she said. "Maybe we could . . . go to the movies?"

Fernando considered, then nodded. "All right." Then his tone became firm. "Follow me." He led Ann around the corner into a quiet alley, picked up a stick, and, in a patch of dirt, sketched a rough map of the city — really just a circle with a couple of diagonal lines through it.

"We have to get organized. Now, here we are," he said, making an *X* in the dirt.

What a good idea, Ann thought. It makes us seem like explorers or gangsters.

"We'll need food. Did you bring your lunch, Ann? Good. So did I. Do you have any money?" Fernando was becoming very businesslike.

"A little," Ann answered. Her mother always made her carry two dollars with her as "emergency money," to be used for food or buses or telephone calls. Ann had always thought this was silly, but now she saw that it could come in handy. "Do you have any?"

Fernando nodded. "We'll need water, too. But we can drink at the fountains in the park . . . if they don't run out."

Ann took the stick and pointed. "Let's proceed north-northeast down James Street until we get to the park. We can make camp there and decide on further maneuvers." She was getting into the mood of the adventure. She didn't know if the direction was really north-northeast, but it had always been her favorite: it sounded so rugged.

Fernando agreed and traced their path on his map. Then he tossed the stick aside, erased the map carefully with his shoe so that enemies couldn't find it and track them down, and the two set off. It wasn't until later that he wished he had thought to wipe his fingerprints off the stick.

It was a beautiful day in early spring: just windy enough to require a jacket, but sunny enough not to have to zip it up. They wandered slowly down the busy street, stopping to look at each shop window.

"I know, Fernando," Ann said. "Let's decide what we'd buy if we had a lot of money. But we can only pick from things we've seen so far on this street. What would you get?"

"I'd get that grand piano," Fernando said. "That way I could practice at home."

Ann thought for a moment. "I think I'd get that camera and the extra equipment that goes with it for making your own pictures. Then I could work in my laboratory at night and become a great photographer."

"Wait, that set of pots and pans was really good, too." Fernando hesitated. "But if I got that, I wouldn't have enough money for the piano."

"Well," Ann said, "if we were rich we could put our money together and get all three things."

"I guess we could." Fernando glanced up and down the street, then leaned over to whisper confidentially in Ann's ear. "That was a close one, Ann. They almost saw us."

"Who?"

"Didn't you see that red car? Every red car is filled with teachers on the lookout for people skipping school. And if they catch us, they . . ."

Ann was eager to add to the new game. "If they catch us, we have to do self-expression plays for the whole school."

At the approach of each red car, the two ran to flatten themselves in doorways, holding their breath with suspense. When the danger had passed, they laughed and wiped their brows with relief.

They relished their newfound freedom, delicious because forbidden. The passersby, the buildings, and the traffic held a new and special charm because it was all happening at a time when they ought to be in school. They were sampling the life adults had set aside for themselves.

When they arrived at the park, Ann and Fernando sat down at the edge of the pond and ate their lunches, throwing pieces of bread from their sandwiches to the ducks. The sunlight shone down through the rustling treetops, and Ann was suddenly struck by how happy she was.

"I wish that the whole fifth-grade class," she said dreamily, "could be flushed down a huge toilet." Then she added, "Except for us."

"Except for us and Mark," Fernando corrected. Mark was his best friend.

"All right, but the rest have to go."

As they talked on, it occurred to Ann that she really did have a friend after all — Fernando. It's a pity he's a boy, she thought. Or maybe the real pity is that people like Patty and Suzy tease girls for being friends with boys. But as long as they don't know about it, we can be great friends. Secrets are more fun, anyway.

"Fernando," Ann asked after a long silence during which they each followed their own daydreams, "do you ever worry about what you'll be when you grow up?"

"Worry?"

"Well, I mean . . . Do you think about it?"

"Yes. I want to be a chef in a restaurant like my uncle."

"Oh? Is that why you wanted those pots and pans?"

"Yeah. It's very important to work with good utensils," he said seriously. "Sometimes after school I go over to where my uncle works and he lets me cut vegetables and do easy things. And I cook dinner at home sometimes, too. Last week I made *coq au vin*."

"Really?" Ann wasn't exactly sure what that was, but it sounded very fancy and complicated. How much fun it was to be lounging on the grass in the middle of a school day, talking about exotic foreign foods! The sun, wind, adventure, companionship — everything was perfect. I hope I'll always remember this day, Ann thought. Maybe when I have children who hate school, I'll suggest this very thing to them. Go ahead, I'll say. If school is too bad, go to the park and feed the ducks. But watch out for red cars. Perhaps I will have forgotten what it's like to be a child by then. No, I don't think I will. I'll still remember. I won't forget. I won't forget. Ann's daydreams grew singsong with laziness and happiness.

"Come on, Ann," Fernando said, getting back to business. "It's time for the second part of our mission." He drew a new map and squinted at it professionally. "From here we'll circle around the park once. That way we'll throw anyone who might be following us off the track. Then we'll go south on Manchester until we get to the Saxon."

"South-southwest," Ann corrected.

Fernando shrugged. "Okay."

Before long the two stood on the busy corner in front of the Saxon Theatre and saw on the marquee that they were just in time for the early matinee of a foreign film. When they counted out their money carefully, they found they had only enough for one ticket. Fernando checked all his pockets again, then sat on the curb looking worried.

"Well, Ann, maybe we can do something else," he suggested.

But Ann was determined to go to the movies. There must be no disappointments on this perfect day. She took the situation in hand.

"You go ahead, Fernando," she said.

"I don't want to go alone," he protested.

"You take the money and go in. I'll be in later,"

"But how can —"

"I'll see you in five minutes," she said firmly.

Fernando took the money rather doubtfully and did as Ann had directed. She sat on the curb for a few minutes to give him a head start and to work up courage for the daring plan that had occurred to her. She knew that she was small and looked younger than her age. This had always bothered her, but today she saw that it would have its advantages. What she was planning would be a blow to her dignity, but it had to be done.

Ann jumped up and ran past the ticket booth to the doors of the theater.

"Mommy!" she cried, pressing her face against the glass.

"Where's your ticket?" the woman in the booth called out with irritation.

"Mommy! Mommy!" Ann screamed, ignoring

the question, as passersby on the street stopped to see why this little girl was so distressed.

"You need a ticket if you want to see the show," the woman insisted rather nervously.

"My mommy's in there!" Ann screamed wildly, and she pretended to cry.

"Oh, for . . . All right!" the woman said with exasperation. "Go on in!"

Ann tugged open the door and tiptoed through the lobby. She had never been in this huge, old-fashioned theater before. It was a beautiful room with very tall, intricately carved pillars on both ends reaching up to a ceiling covered with plaster angels and flowers. A round stained-glass window was reflected in an enormous mirror with a gold frame on the opposite wall, and little circles of gem-colored light danced on the plush carpet. This is a palace for a princess, Ann thought, only it smells like popcorn. She frowned at the shabby refreshment counter in one corner. That shouldn't be allowed, she decided. It spoils the effect.

Ann brushed through a heavy velvet curtain smelling of dust and walked into the theater. When her eyes adjusted to the dark, she saw that it was almost empty. She walked down the sticky aisle and sat down next to Fernando just as the titles of the film came onto the screen.

"Ann," he whispered, "how did you do it?"

The note of admiration in his voice pleased her

greatly. I really am quite smart, she told herself happily. But she believed that if she admitted that she had got in by pretending to be an abandoned child, the caper would seem a little less glamorous.

"I just did," she answered casually. "Sh-h-h."

The movie was in Italian with English subtitles. Ann thought with a pang of guilt that if she had continued her project with the Italian flash cards, she wouldn't need to read what they were saying. But she could understand one or two words that began with A, and that was better than nothing.

It was a story about a cruel circus man who took a girl away from her family and forced her to be a clown. They traveled all around Italy together in a little truck and stopped in towns to perform. The girl had to beat a drum while the man broke chains wrapped around his chest by flexing his muscles, and if the girl played the drum the wrong way, the man hit her. When she got sick, he left her sleeping by a rock. Then a lady hanging up ghostly white laundry told him that the girl had died, and the man went to the beach that night and cried. Ann cried too, but very carefully and quietly so Fernando wouldn't notice. The music was especially lovely and sad, and Ann hoped she would never forget it. She knew this was the best movie she had ever seen. In fact, she had never had any idea that movies could be so touching and good. When it was over and the lights came on she felt dazed, and the nearly empty theater, which had seemed so ornate before, now seemed drab and dead in comparison with the vivid world in the film.

At the lobby door she took Fernando's arm.

"Maybe we'd better run," she warned him, remembering the ticket seller she had tricked.

They flew out of the theater and ran, hopped, and skipped by turns all the way home. At his corner, Fernando turned and shouted without slowing down, "Good-bye, Ann. I'll see you Monday."

That's right! she thought gleefully. It's Friday, and there's no school tomorrow. Then she saw on a church clock that it was exactly the right time for her to be coming home from school. Everything had worked out perfectly. Ann's happiness was complete: for once, fate was on her side.

CHAPTER FOUR

A Month of Sundays

On Sunday afternoon Mother tapped lightly on Ann's door.

"Ann? It's time to get ready to go over to the Sternbergs'. Why don't you put on that nice orange dress you wore the other day? Hurry now."

Ann listened to her mother's retreating footsteps with a dark scowl. She had stayed in her room, bored and restless, all day. Sundays shouldn't be allowed, she decided. Why couldn't there be two Saturdays instead? Even two Mondays would be better, despite Miss Delray and her stupid "learning opportunities." Sunday everything was heavy and messy and somber. The house was littered with dirty coffee cups and depressing, fat newspapers; Ann's parents and sister lounged around in pajamas and bathrobes until lunchtime; and meals were casually thrown together at irregular hours. The lack of order and discipline upset Ann. In an effort to combat it, she always woke up early, dressed promptly, and tried to pretend it was a day like any other while she ate her breakfast alone, everything neatly set out on one end of the table. But by midmorning the emptiness of the streets and the drone of the neighbors' radios always plunged her into a state of inescapable gloom.

And beyond all the natural dreariness of Sunday, the thought of her homework always weighed heavily as well. She never seemed able to force herself to get to it before the last minute on Sunday night, but she let it nag at her all day from the moment she got up.

Once Ann heard the expression "a month of Sundays" and nearly fainted at the thought. But if there was one thing she hated more than Sundays, it was going to the Sternbergs'. Just because Mother liked Mrs. Sternberg, she expected Ann to like Mrs. Sternberg's daughter, Marie. That was not the case. Marie was a doughy, dull girl. She loved to put records on the stereo and sing along with them, swaying gently. She spent hours in front of the mirror inventing exotic hairdos and saying things like "Her lips were as bright as cherries." Worst of all, her idea of a snack was a spoonful of mayonnaise straight from the jar. Ann wondered grimly how many precious days had been ruined by visits to the Sternbergs. She made a vow never to force her own children to play

with her friends' children. It was simply too unfair. After all, Father never had to go and talk to
Mr. Sternberg. In fact, Ann had once overheard
him say, "I can't stand those people. He's a fool,
his wife's a bore, and their kid is spoiled." But
Ann's objections to Marie made no difference to
her mother. All this will be different when I'm a
mother, Ann promised herself. And that made
two things she had to remember for her own
children. Maybe I should make a list, she thought.
No! Better yet, I'll write a book called *Rules About
Bringing Up Children.* Every day I'll think of a new
rule and I'll — Ann froze. She pictured a half-
finished pamphlet lying on the floor of her wardrobe on top of the hammer and nails. THE PILE.
No, Ann thought savagely, I'm not adding to THE
PILE. I'd rather sign up as a school cook right now!

She threw open the door of her wardrobe.
Wearing that orange dress was out of the question. What would do for *little Ann, the humble step-
daughter* would not do for regular Ann. She looked
glumly through her clothes. Unlike Isabelle, she
didn't have many dresses because she had never
liked to dress up. She didn't care for any of the
ones she had particularly, but there were certain
ones she felt like biting to shreds, that orange thing
being at the top of the list.

A few minutes later, Ann appeared in the living room defiantly wearing tennis shoes, old cor-

duroy pants, and a red shirt. She noticed with irritation that Isabelle was wearing a cute little sailor suit and black patent leather shoes.

"Ann, I thought you were going to wear that orange dress you like so," Mother said.

"It was dirty," Ann lied.

"Then put on another one. Hurry, dear."

"I don't have any others," Ann muttered.

"Of course you do, Ann," Mother said impatiently. "Don't be silly."

Isabelle jumped from her chair. "Don't worry, Annie. I'll help you find something pretty, and then you'll look as nice as I do."

That was too much. It was bad enough to have a fight with Mother in front of Isabelle without her playing the calm, helpful little sister.

"I hate my dresses! And I hate that dull pig, Marie!" she shouted as she ran from the room.

Mother and Isabelle left without her.

Ann threw herself onto her bed and slept for a long time, a heavy, troubled sleep. When she awoke it was dark, and she wandered, sleepy, hot, and very hungry, down to the kitchen, where Mother was just finishing the dishes.

"Oh, here you are, darling," Mother exclaimed. "You were sleeping so soundly I didn't wake you for dinner. Would you like some now?"

"All right," Ann said.

"Why don't we go shopping sometime next week

and find you some pretty clothes?" Mother suggested, lighting the flame under the soup.

"No, that's okay," Ann said guiltily. Actually, her clothes weren't all that bad.

"But we haven't been out shopping together for a long time. I'm ahead of schedule in my work, and I can afford to take an afternoon off. It would be fun."

That was true. Clothing expeditions with Mother were among life's treats.

"Okay." Happily, Ann began to eat her soup. I really do have a very nice mother, she thought.

Mother sat down at the table with Ann. "How is school?" she asked. "Are you learning interesting things?"

"No. It's terrible," Ann said, smiling. She told about Miss Delray's play, imitating her teacher's silly affectations, and Mother laughed and explained to her the nonsense of progressive education. As they chatted, Ann realized how much she liked talking to her parents one at a time. Sometimes they seemed like one bland team of Parenthood, and it was easy to forget that they were two distinct people who at some time in the distant past didn't even *know* one another.

"Are you enjoying your new room?" Mother asked.

Ann hesitated. She hadn't told her parents about the dreams she'd had the first nights. It seemed babyish to have nightmares, and she was afraid that her parents might make her sleep with Isabelle again.

"Oh, I like it fine," she said vaguely.

"And you're not frightened up there all alone?"

It wouldn't be a bit frightening if I *were* all alone, Ann thought uneasily, remembering the little waving figure and the carnival.

"No," she said quickly, "I really like it. Well, I'm going up to do my homework now. Goodnight." She kissed her mother and started slowly up the stairs. As she mounted, uneasiness became fear. It wasn't that the dream was really terrifying in itself. The little girl prompted more pity than dread. But both times Ann had been left feeling horribly guilty for not recognizing her and not being willing to accompany her.

Ann stopped in the middle of the attic stairs, turned around, and walked into Isabelle's room.

Isabelle was sitting on the floor, playing school with her favorite doll, Segeener, as the teacher and her teddy bears arranged in a semicircle as the attentive students. Is that all she ever does? Ann thought with annoyance. She should study. That girl hardly knows her alphabet, and I bet she can't name one country in Africa.

"Don't you have any homework?" Ann asked severely.

"I'm too young for homework," Isabelle said.

"And my teddies don't have homework either. Do you want to play with Segeener and me?"

"No, I don't want to play," Ann said scornfully. Actually, it looked like fun, but Ann had come with a different purpose in mind. She had noticed that she was always less frightened when she was with someone even more scared than she.

"Isabelle, I just read a really scary book," Ann began, sitting down on the edge of the bed that had once been hers but that now held more than twenty of Isabelle's dolls and teddies.

"Really?" Isabelle made a silly, high voice for Segeener's role as teacher. "Ann just read a really scary book, class."

"Yeah. I wasn't scared by it, though," Ann continued casually. "It was mostly about wolves."

"Wolves?" Isabelle was terribly afraid of wolves.

"Yes, wolves. They were special wolves that only attacked little girls, and they ran so fast that the girls could hardly see them until it was too late."

Isabelle set Segeener aside numbly.

"It was really very interesting," Ann continued matter-of-factly. "You see, the wolves grow like mushrooms in little girls' closets . . ."

Isabelle quickly looked over at her closet.

". . . and then, at night, they creep out and cast a spell over the girls so they can't move. They can see the wolves coming slowly, with their green eyes shining in the dark, but they can't move a muscle."

After a breathless silence, Isabelle asked faintly, "But it was just a story, right?"

Ann shrugged. "Who knows?" she said lightly.

There was another short silence. "Annie," Isabelle began eagerly, "do you want to sleep here tonight? We could pretend Segeener was sick and give her medicine and everything, and it would really be fun!"

Ann's plan had worked. Now that Isabelle was truly terrified, Ann felt quite brave. "No, thanks. I think I'll sleep in my own room." As she left, she called over her shoulder, "You'd better shut that closet door."

Ann whipped through her homework in no time at all. As always, what she had dreaded all day had turned out to be very easy. Ann knew perfectly well that doing things was easier than thinking and worrying about them, but knowing didn't seem to help much. She still put things off, and she still worried about them. She hoped this was one of those things children are supposed to outgrow.

At last Sunday was over. Ann looked around her neat, cozy bedroom, and she realized her fear of the dream had disappeared. Sometimes I'm almost as silly as Isabelle, she thought, suddenly feeling a pang of remorse for the mean way she had scared her. Ann went back downstairs and opened Isabelle's door softly.

"Isabelle?" she said.

Her sister had not budged since Ann left, and she shrieked at the sound of Ann's voice.

"Oh, it's you," she quavered, wild-eyed.

"I forgot to tell you. It said in the story that those wolves never grow in closets that have a red dress in them. They hate red dresses so much that they won't even come near a house where there's one."

"But, Annie, *I* have a red dress in *my* closet!" Isabelle shouted happily. She ran to show her sister.

"Oh, is that so? Well, the wolves couldn't possibly be in yours, then." Ann spoke as though the very idea was absurd. "Goodnight, Isabelle."

As she left, she heard Isabelle cheerfully continuing her game. I'm such a good sister, Ann thought smugly.

From that day on, Isabelle was very careful to hang her red dress up neatly in her closet. She hung up all her other dresses too, just for good measure.

Mother praised her for becoming tidier.

CHAPTER FIVE

Lily

O n Monday morning Ann walked to school in her favorite method. From the bottom step of her stoop she took a giant leap and landed with both feet on the nearest crack in the sidewalk. Then she started with her left foot placed carefully in the middle of the next slab of pavement. The right foot landed squarely on the next crack. And so she went, all the way to school: left middle, right crack, left middle, right crack. Once, in the second grade, she had experimented with putting her left foot on the cracks, but she had found that this felt deeply wrong. Her head bowed in concentration, she strode to the end of the block. Crossing streets was a different matter. Getting safely across was more important than keeping up the routine; anyway, most streets had no cracks, and it was impossible to jump from one curb to the next. Still, it bothered Ann to have to break the perfect pattern at all. Streets just don't count, in crack-walking, she assured herself firmly.

It was three blocks from her house that the real crack-walking challenge began. Because of various repairs to the sidewalk, the cracks appeared at irregular intervals. Sometimes they were so far apart that she had to take enormous steps to make it across in two strides. Other times, the gaps between cracks were so small that she had to take tiny tiptoe steps to fit two in. One small patch of brick was particularly difficult. Children less sensitive to the need for exact, tidy routines might have pretended that brick sidewalks, like streets, didn't count, but Ann knew in her heart that they did, and that a walk like this was only truly satisfying if it was done absolutely correctly.

Because crack-walking was notably slower than normal walking, the tardy bell rang when Ann was only halfway across the playground. Now came the moment of decision . . .

Should Ann, world-class crack-walker, ruin her international reputation by running sloppily the rest of the way just so she wouldn't be late for school? Never! Not even if all the teachers were watching her slow approach from behind their windows! Nothing would stand between her and perfection. After so many other failures in her life, she would rather face the cruelest torture than go back on what she believed. Her motto was: "Life is not always easy."

Filled with cool determination, she continued

her left middle, right crack walk all the way down the hall to the door of her classroom. She arrived late but triumphant.

The first thing she noticed was Fernando standing at Mrs. Weed's desk with a piece of paper in his hand. Of course! It was his excuse for being absent Friday. It seemed like such a long time ago that Ann had completely forgotten about bringing a note. But how did Fernando have one? Had he told his parents what they had done?

As she made her way to her desk, Ann caught his eye with a questioning look.

"My sister," he whispered as she passed.

Oh, yes. Fernando had an older sister in high school who could fake his mother's handwriting quite easily. Some people had all the luck. Ann tried to imagine the kind of note Isabelle would be able to write for her: a page filled with long lines of the meaningless scribble that Isabelle called "my writing." What a useless girl she was!

Then, looking around the room, Ann got her second surprise of the morning. There was a new girl in the class. She had long dark hair tied in a braid down her back and she wore — Ann noticed with a combination of disapproval and envy — gold hoop earrings. The new girl turned her dark eyes on Ann and watched her steadily.

"Ann? Do you have a note? Ann?" Mrs. Weed's voice cut in suddenly.

"Uh . . . No, Mrs. Weed. I forgot it," Ann replied weakly.

"Make sure you bring it tomorrow," Mrs. Weed said.

Oh my, Ann thought. A note. Oh no.

As the morning wore on, Ann was aware of the new girl's gaze upon her. It's very hard not to look back at someone who is staring at you, so their eyes met often, but Ann was always the first to look away and busy herself with her papers.

During lunch Ann learned about the new girl. She had come to school for the first time on Friday, her name was Lily, and, most interesting of all, she was twelve years old. Now that Ann had had her birthday, all the children in the class were either ten or eleven. It seemed awfully strange to be twelve and only in the fifth grade, and stranger yet to wear gold hoop earrings. However, when Patty Dorval voiced her hissing disapproval, Ann decided that she liked the earrings — and the girl wearing them, too.

In the middle of history class that afternoon, Ann noticed that a small piece of paper was making its way across the room. Each time the teacher looked at the blackboard, the note was thrust quickly into the hand of the next student, who read it, turned to stare at Ann, then snickered. They're passing a note about me, Ann thought with a feeling of doom. This wasn't the first time it had happened, and Ann reminded herself that it didn't matter what these insignificant people thought of her, but still she felt both embarrassment and frustrated rage. Once a note had been about Ann's misbuttoned sweater. She gave her clothing a rapid check now, but she could see nothing wrong. It must be something worse, she thought.

The note had begun in the first row and was moving toward the back of the room. Ann sat roughly in the middle, so it was some consolation to know that she might be able to stop this thing halfway through. She waited patiently and returned each leer with a cool look. When Beth, who sat in front of Ann, had the note and was about to pass it around her, Ann dropped her pencil on the floor, leaned forward to pick it up, and with a quick snatch tore the note from Beth's hand. Slowly she unfolded it on her lap. Written in Patty Dorval's unmistakable hand, as round and squat as she was, it read: "Isn't it funny how Ann and Fernando were *both* absent Friday?" And there was a large heart with an arrow through it.

Ann's own heart sank, and she was furious to find herself blushing hotly. A general giggle proved that the class had noticed her glowing cheeks. She raged inside. By blushing she had given away the fact that their absence was not just coincidence. Nothing could be worse. The old rumor was given new life, and it promised to flourish more threateningly than before. Ann tore the note into tiny bits and let them flutter gracefully to the floor, wishing every second that the paper was Patty's plump body. She was thankful that she had destroyed the note before Fernando saw it and was forced to share her embarrassment.

After school, Ann found a gang waiting for her on the playground. Patty, Suzy, Beth, Mike Dunk — all her worst enemies were there, whispering among themselves and smirking.

"Hi, Ann," Patty began in a jeering voice. "We were just saying it's kind of funny that you and Fernando were both absent on Friday."

"Oh, do you think so?" Ann asked.

"Well, I mean . . . You know what I mean."

"Yes, I read your little note," Ann said with grim dignity.

"I bet you they were" — Patty finished her sentence by whispering loudly into Suzy's ear — "kissing."

The group burst into laughter, and Ann's temper suddenly snapped.

"Yes! Yes!" she screamed. "It's true! I love Fernando! And Fernando loves me! We are very, very happy!"

Ann stopped, aghast. What was she saying? Piercing screams of laughter greeted her declaration. Would she have to change schools? Suddenly she felt a slim arm around her shoulders. Ann spun in surprise and saw that it was the new girl, Lily. Lily addressed the group calmly in a low, mysterious voice.

"Those who mock what they do not understand are severely punished. Love is rare and beautiful. I can only hope that one day you will be as fortunate as Ann, and that you will be forgiven for your ignorance."

The gossipers stared in disbelief.

"Come on, Ann," Lily said quietly, leading her away. Before Ann had time to know what was happening and thank the strange girl, Lily had left her standing alone and had disappeared into the throng on the playground. Ann felt dizzy.

That evening in her attic room Ann laid down her pen and surveyed her work:

Dear Mrs. Weed:
    Please excuse Ann's absence on
Friday. She was sick.
                                Sincerely yours,

This was her fifth attempt at imitating her mother's handwriting. It was no use. Ann's writing was loopy and her mother's was spiky. At best, the note looked like something Ann had written on a moving train. It would never fool Mrs. Weed. Spiky writing shouldn't be allowed!

The door to Ann's room opened suddenly, and she crumpled up the paper guiltily.

"Hi, Annie. What are you doing?" Isabelle asked.

"Get out of here! Don't ever come into my room without knocking!" Ann shouted.

Isabelle's happy face began to crumple. "I can come in if I want to. It's my house too. And if you don't stop being so mean, I'll tell Mommy and you'll get in a lot of trouble!"

"*Get out!*" Ann bellowed. Isabelle stuck out her lower lip and stamped away while Ann returned to the enormous problem at hand. What if I tell Mrs. Weed that I had a note but Isabelle ate it? I could say that . . . No, that wouldn't work. With a sigh, Ann climbed into bed and put the pillow over her head to keep the world out.

"Don't you recognize me?"

This time the voice in her dream was shrill and accusing. Ann dreamt she awoke and lay perfectly still on her bed in the darkness. The wind ruffled the papers on the desk and filled the curtains like sails.

I am *not* going to the window, Ann told herself. I'm going to stay right here. She closed her eyes tightly and pleaded for it all to go away. She knew what would happen next, and she felt her stomach grow cold with fright when it did. The carnival sounds filtered in, and over the music the voice was clear and piercing.

"Come with me, Ann. Hurry," it demanded.

Tense with her effort to resist but unable to, she began to glide across the floor toward the window. The moist wind flowed over her body as she placed her fingertips on the glass and gazed down at the figure standing by the eerily lit merry-go-round. All wrapped in shawls and scarves, it looked rather like a little Gypsy, but Ann could not see the face.

Then a frightening thing happened. The wind that had been blowing into the room suddenly changed direction and began pulling Ann out the window! The force was so great that she had to lock her knees and brace herself against the frame to keep from being swept right through the glass and down to the ground below.

"Come, Ann," the Gypsy called.

Ann's nightgown billowed straight out in front of her, and the curtains flapped crazily through the glass against the rough brick outer wall. As the force grew stronger, Ann's arms began to tremble with the effort of holding herself in. She felt herself growing weak; her hands were sweaty with panic, and she felt herself slipping.

"No, no!" she screamed.

Abruptly, the wind stopped, the carnival lights disappeared, the music ceased. And the Gypsy was gone.

When Ann woke up she was staring, her round eyes filled with tears, down into the dark back garden.

Weak and shaking with fear and fatigue, she crept back into bed and cried herself to sleep.

CHAPTER SIX

A Miraculous Recovery

Ann awoke with a feeling of utter doom. Everything filled her with dread, and she felt helpless to struggle against her fate.

Life was black, black, black.

As she lay in the rumpled bed, too miserable to move, she tried weakly to review her desperate situation. Even in this grim task she was orderly. To begin with, she told herself, everything is terrible. I can divide my disasters into three groups: School, Career, and . . . Other. Ann made an outline in her head the way Mrs. Weed had taught her to do for compositions.

 I. School.
  A. I hate school.
   1. It is boring.
   2. It is stupid.
  B. I hate all the people in school.

      1. Except Mrs. Weed.

      2. And Fernando.

      3. And maybe Lily.

C. Everyone hates me.

      1. Mrs. Weed will hate me when she finds out I don't have an excuse for Friday.

      2. Fernando will hate me when he finds out what I said on the playground.

      3. Lily will probably join the others who have always hated me and always will.

         a. Though I don't care!

D. I don't have a note for being absent.

      1. I'll probably get sent to the principal and be thrown out of school.

      2. Then I'll never go to college.

         a. And I'll end up a school cook!

II. Career.

A. By now I should have already chosen a career and I should be devoting myself to it slavishly.

      1. By my age, Mozart was almost over the hill.

      2. But all I've got to show for my life is THE PILE!

B. I am smart.

1. Therefore, I am almost sure that if I could only force myself to work hard on one thing I could become good at it.
2. The reason I fail at all my projects must be that I am lazy and spoiled.
3. Maybe I'd be happier if I weren't smart.
4. With my luck, I'd probably end up both dumb *and* unhappy.

C. I am running out of time.

1. If I don't get to work soon I'll never be great and famous.
2. Maybe it's already too late!

III. Other.

A. This category is too big and too ghastly to think about!

B. For one thing, nobody can be great and famous without a good night's sleep, and I can't get one because I'm afraid and I keep having bad dreams!

1. Maybe I'm sleepwalking.
2. What if I fall out of the window one night?
   a. Yes, then what?
3. Then I'll *really* never go to college!
4. If I don't get any sleep, I'll prob-

          ably get sick and no one at school
will care because they hate me.
5. Maybe I'll die.
     a. At least then I won't have to
       worry about my career.
C. Why am I so mean to Isabelle?
1. Because she's a pest?
2. Because she's silly and messy?
3. Because she never worries about
  her future?

Ann had to stop thinking because she was working herself into a frenzy. Everything was all too dark and terrible. Furthermore, she couldn't keep track of whether she was on a roman numeral or a letter or a number. Her troubles were simply too many and too vast to be organized neatly.

Mother called again for her to get up and get ready for school. Through all this turmoil one fact, at least, was clear: going to school today was impossible. She had to pretend to be sick. She waited until she heard her mother coming up the stairs, then she scrubbed her face hard with her hands, jumped out of bed, spun in tiny circles until she could barely stand, and reeled back into bed just as Mother opened the door.

"Ann, didn't you hear me calling? You're going to be late. Breakfast is ready."

"Oh," Ann said in her faintest voice. "Mother, I don't feel very well."

"What's wrong, darling?" Mother sat on the edge of the bed and put her hand on Ann's forehead. "You do look rather flushed."

That face-rubbing really works, Ann thought. "I have a headache. And I feel sort of hot and . . . dizzy," she said truthfully.

"You stay here. I'll go get the thermometer," Mother said.

Ann sighed with relief. The hardest part was over. She only wished that she hadn't spun quite so hard, because she really did feel very queasy. And it worried her to skip school again. What if the class started some new complicated math today? What if she could never catch up? I'll probably flunk the fifth grade, she thought sadly.

Little Ann was a sickly girl. Her fragile health prevented her from realizing her potential. She would surely have become a great scientist and artist, but she failed the fifth grade.

Mother came back with the thermometer, put it under Ann's tongue, and hurried away to send Isabelle off to school.

Ann knew all about thermometers. She took this one out of her mouth as soon as her mother left. Long ago she had learned that it's risky to use artificial means to make thermometers hotter — such as scrubbing the bulb on the bottom against the blankets — because it's difficult to control how hot they get. And mothers grow suspicious when they read one hundred ten. It's much safer to make them too cool. Then mothers worry that their children are weak and about to get sick. Ann put the thermometer back into her mouth just before her mother returned.

"Let's see now," Mother said. "Well, you don't have a fever, but your temperature is well under normal. It might be best for you to stay home today and rest. You could be on the verge of an illness."

"Oh, but I . . . Oh, all right." Ann struggled to keep the triumph out of her voice.

By noon, Ann was totally, unspeakably bored.

She wandered downstairs and heard her mother and father laughing in the kitchen. This surprised her. She hadn't known that Father came home from the university for lunch. What do they talk about when Isabelle and I aren't around? she wondered. It must be dull for them without us.

"Well, hello, dear," Father said. "I hear you're feeling under the weather."

"Do you think you're well enough to come down?" Mother asked.

"Yes, I feel a little better," Ann said guiltily.

"My poor daughter is unwell. How would it be

if I brought you home a treat tonight, honey?"
Father asked.

"Uh . . No, that's okay," Ann said, feeling even
more guilty. Parents really knew how to make a
girl feel ashamed.

"Could you eat a little something?" Mother
asked.

"I'll try," Ann promised bravely. She seated
herself at the table and ate ravenously.

"At least your appetite seems good," Father re-
marked.

Ann couldn't stand it any longer. "I'm not really
sick," she blurted out.

Her parents looked at her in confusion.

"I . . . I skipped school on Friday and went to
the movies instead." There! She had said it. Ann
braced herself for the storm that would follow.

"Why?" her mother asked.

"Because school is dull and all we do are stupid
plays and everybody hates me and I don't have
any friends and . . ." She could feel the hot tears
rising in her eyes.

"Have you skipped school often?" Father asked
in a serious voice.

"No! Only this once." Ann was shocked at the
very thought. "Then yesterday I didn't have an
excuse for Mrs. Weed, so I . . ."

"I see," Mother said. Then both parents

launched into a lecture about how it was Ann's duty to go to school. It was her job, just as writing was her mother's job and teaching her father's, and Ann should not take her job lightly. They could imagine that the teachers weren't always the best, and they realized that children could be cruel, but nevertheless . . .

It might be better if they'd just spank me, Ann thought.

But Father ended the lecture on a surprisingly cheerful note. "However, since your grades are always good, and you seem to like learning even if you don't always like school, I don't see why we should take this matter too seriously. After all, it's only a first offense on a spotless record. But in the future, darling, please go to school."

Ann realized with amazement that both her parents were smiling. How lucky I am, she thought, to have such reasonable parents. They aren't even going to punish me. And Father even confessed that he had skipped school once or twice when the going got too dull.

"But, Ann," Mother said, "I think you really may be a little unwell. You didn't look very good this morning. Maybe you had better lie down again. The world always looks bleak and things seem impossible when you aren't feeling your best."

Ann felt a bit uncomfortable and dishonest. This

would be the perfect time for a full confession, but she didn't think she should go as far as telling her parents about her method of producing instant illness. How could she be sure she wouldn't need to use that trick again sometime? To ease her conscience, she vowed she would tell them all about it as soon as she was in college and well away from people like Patty and Suzy and Miss Delray.

"I feel much better now," she said, smiling.

"You're sure?"

"Yes."

"Well, in that case, today might be as good a day as any to go on that shopping trip we planned," Mother said.

Ann laughed aloud with surprise. Far from being punished, she was being given the treat of a shopping trip! Ann promised herself she would never play hookey again.

The shopping trip was a great success. Mother and daughter chatted happily as they went in and out of stores and later over chocolate malteds in a pretty pink and white ice cream parlor downtown. Now that Ann had confessed to skipping school, the other things that had been bothering her melted into the background. She discovered that when one problem has been solved, the others seem less threatening. She also discovered that new clothes work wonders in lifting the spirits.

She came home with a bag containing a beautiful dark green dress with a white collar and cuffs and three pairs of dazzlingly white knee socks. She rushed right up to her room to put everything on and show her father, who was gratifyingly impressed by her beauty.

While Ann was undressing, Isabelle burst in. "Hi, Annie! Are you — "

"Don't ever come into my room without knocking," Ann said with automatic anger.

"Sorry." Isabelle went back out and knocked softly.

"Yes? Who's there?" Ann asked.

"It's me!"

"Who?"

"Isabelle!"

"What do you want?"

"May I come in?"

"Well . . . if you must."

"Hi, Annie!" Isabelle said, entering. "Are you feeling better?"

The question annoyed Ann deeply, because it touched on the one unpleasant aspect of a perfect day: her deception of her mother.

"Yes," she said curtly.

"Is that a new dress?" Isabelle asked, her eyes wide. Pretty clothes were Isabelle's greatest passion.

"Mother took me shopping. And I got new

socks, too," Ann said proudly as she tugged the dress off over her head.

"Oh-h." Isabelle looked puzzled. Her own days spent sick at home never led to shopping trips. "That's a really pretty dress."

"Yes, I know. Mother gave it to me for being a particularly good girl."

Later that evening, Ann passed Isabelle's room and looked in to see her prancing in front of her mirror wearing a blue dress with Ann's silk dresser scarf draped around her shoulders like a shawl. She looked very pretty.

"Don't you ever take my things again without asking me first!" Ann hissed. She yanked the dresser scarf from her sister's shoulders and slapped her.

"I just wanted to make my dress look prettier," Isabelle explained tearfully. "Anyway, it isn't fair. It isn't fair! *I* never get dresses when *I'm* sick. Just because you're smart in school, you get everything!"

Ann stalked away, ashamed of her unreasonable treatment of Isabelle. And angry with Isabelle for making her feel so ashamed.

On her pillow she found a note:

Dear Mrs. Weed:
Please excuse Ann's absence from

school on Friday. She was feverish, so I
thought it best to keep her at home.
Tuesday she seemed to suffer a slight
relapse, but I am confident that she is
now completely recovered.

Sincerely,

There it was, complete with the genuine spiky
signature. Now there would be no need to see the
principal. Ann was back on the road to college
. . . and success . . . and fame.

I must remember to write my children lots and
lots of absence notes, Ann thought. Maybe even
some spare ones to use whenever they need them.
It wouldn't really be bad because my children will
be like me and they won't skip school unless it's
really necessary. For the second time that day,
Ann marveled at the kindness and wisdom of her
parents, and she decided to pay them back by
being a better daughter.

Being a better daughter . . . Ann thought of
Isabelle and the scarf and the slap, and she felt
weak with remorse. She knew that she could best
be a better daughter by being a better sister. Why,
she asked herself miserably, *why* did I have to be
so mean to Isabelle on a day when my parents
were so nice to me? I don't even need that old
silk scarf.

I don't have a dresser to put it on!

CHAPTER SEVEN

The Reading

During the next few days at school, Ann was very much aware of Lily's presence. It seemed that each time she looked up from her work, Lily's eyes were on her; and even when she didn't look up, she could feel the pressure of Lily's gaze, a sort of tingling at the back of her neck. Ann knew that she should speak to Lily, at least to thank her for her support on the playground, but she felt shy about the incident. In truth, she would rather forget that horribly embarrassing afternoon altogether. Nevertheless, Lily had come to her rescue and did deserve some thanks, particularly since her low voice and penetrating stare had been so effective that not even Patty Dorval had so much as mentioned Fernando to Ann afterward. And Fernando seemed to be his normal, friendly self, so Ann could only guess that no one had told him about her rash declaration of love.

Everyone seemed to be a little afraid of Lily. She was so calm and quiet. And her voice had subtle traces of an accent — more a rhythm of speech than a difference in pronunciation. And she wore gold hoop earrings. And, after all, she *was* twelve.

That Friday, during lunch, Lily asked Ann in a matter-of-fact tone if she would like to come home with her after school. An outsider herself, Ann recognized the casual tone as a protection against rejection, so she accepted the invitation immediately and felt happily excited the rest of the day. It was not often that she was asked over to someone's house, and Lily's house was sure to be interesting.

After school they met and began walking slowly toward a commercial part of town. After a silence, Ann said, "Lily, it was nice of you to stick up for me the other day."

Lily simply closed her eyes and shrugged. That shrug filled Ann with new admiration. What a girl. She could face a whole jeering crowd in a new school and act as though there was nothing to it.

"I'm used to people like that," she said flatly. "Bullies are the same everywhere."

"They're really just cowards, aren't they?"

"Sure. They only feel brave when they have you

outnumbered, and they're usually pretty easy to embarrass." Suddenly Lily laughed. "Hey, Ann, do you remember?" Then she spoke in a deep voice, quivering and melodramatic. "Those who mock what they do not understand are severely punished."

Both girls burst into laughter. It occurred to Ann that there was no surer bond between two people than having enemies in common.

"Even Patty didn't know what to say," Ann said. "And she's always fast to blurt out answers when she's in class."

"Is she the teacher's pet?"

"Well, I don't think she's Mrs. Weed's favorite, but she's Miss Delray's, that's for sure. Miss Delray lets her take attendance and clap the erasers sometimes. And once the class was being noisy, so Miss Delray made everybody write lines except Patty, because she said she knew Patty was too mature to cause trouble." It was a pleasant and novel experience for Ann to talk to someone who was newer to the class than she. For the first time, she was put in the position of being a relative insider. "But I don't think Patty's mature at all. She's just childish and bossy. She thinks she has so many friends, but really Suzy and Beth just follow her around because they're afraid of her and they don't even —" Suddenly Ann fell silent, recognizing in her voice hints of the mean and gossipy way Patty Dorval herself spoke. Insiders sound like insiders, she thought, and it isn't a very pleasant sound. "But, then, Patty *is* the best in reading class," Ann finished.

After they had walked along quietly for a time, Ann said, "Those are pretty earrings. How long have you had pierced ears?"

"Since I was a baby."

"Since you were a baby?"

Lily shrugged. "We all do."

Ann was reluctant to ask who "we" were, though she was wildly curious. "How come you're twelve and only in the fifth grade, Lily?"

"Oh, Mom and I move around so much that I get behind in school."

Her answer fascinated Ann, who had attended the same school since the first grade. "What does your father do?" she asked.

"I don't have a father."

"Oh," Ann said, realizing that that was not an adequate response to so important a revelation. She might have said something like "I'm sorry," but the offhand way in which Lily had spoken prohibited any expression of regret. It was simply a fact, like not having uncles.

They had reached a busy and somewhat run-down part of the city when Lily turned into a doorway between the Beebop Record Shop and Dora's Hairstyling Creations.

"I live here," she said.

Ann looked up at the building and saw a sign on the second floor that read: SISTER ANGELA — READER/ADVISER. Ann envied Lily's living in this exciting downtown neighborhood. On her own street there wasn't a single store, only rows and rows of brick houses. Ann followed Lily up a dark stairway as the heavy glass door shut behind them, muffling the traffic sounds. Lily took a key out of her pocket and opened the door.

"I guess Mom's not home," she said as they entered. "Put your books here and I'll make us something to eat." Lily disappeared through a curtain of glass beads and left Ann staring at the oddest living room she had ever seen.

It was dark and cluttered and colorful, and it smelled rather sweet and spicy. The floor was covered with layers of red, green, and orange rugs that contrasted harshly with an enormous purple velvet sofa. Religious pictures hung so closely together on the walls that it was impossible to determine the color of the paper behind them. Scattered about the room were small tables littered with gilt statues, large ashtrays, candles, artificial flowers, and orange lamps so encrusted with colored glass that they hardly gave off any light.

Ann recognized this as what her mother would consider horrible taste, but she found it exciting and enchanting. Through the yellowed lace curtains, she noticed the back of the sign she had seen from outside.

"Is your mother Sister Angela?" she asked when Lily reappeared with a plate of sandwiches.

"Yeah," Lily said, settling into the purple sofa. "She's a reader."

"A reader? What do you mean?"

"Oh, you know. She reads palms and cards. Sometimes tea leaves. She has the gift."

The Gift? The words had a fascinating and slightly frightening sound to Ann.

"You mean, she can read minds and tell the future?" Ann asked softly.

"Sure." Lily took a bite of her sandwich.

"Can you do it, too?"

Lily shrugged. "A little. But business wasn't too good where we used to live. That's why we moved here."

Business? This girl talks like an adult, Ann thought. How can she take this so calmly? She has a magical mother, and she just sits there eating a peanut butter and jelly sandwich! Ann's head was spinning with more questions when the door opened and in came Sister Angela herself. She was wearing a full skirt, a red blouse, high heels, and enormous earrings. Her long black hair was pulled back in a braid, and her face was heavily made up. So fortunetellers really do look like fortunetellers, Ann thought with wonder.

"Hi, honey, You got a friend over. That's nice." Sister Angela sat down and, with long red fingernails, dragged a cigarette out of her bag.

"Any customers today?" Lily asked.

"Not bad." Sister Angela shrugged and turned to Ann. "And what's your name, honey?"

"Ann," Ann whispered.

"That's a real pretty name. Hey, you want a reading? No charge for Lily's friends."

Ann looked uncertainly toward Lily, who was paying no attention to her, busily painting her fingernails. Painting her fingernails!

"Ah . . . I suppose so," Ann answered shyly.

Sister Angela took Ann's hand and, scarcely glancing at it, began to talk in a rapid monotone.

"You gonna have a good life. You gonna do good in school like you should, and you gonna get a good job. I see travel to distant places. I see here you ain't gonna have no troubles with money. You gonna marry a real nice guy who treats you good. I see two kids. A boy and a girl. I see some happy times and some sad times. But don't you worry, honey, because the happy times are gonna win out in the end. If you are true to yourself, everything's gonna work out fine. I see gold and silver. And you gonna take a trip in a boat . . ."

Sister Angela's voice trailed off as she frowned and pulled Ann's hand closer to her eyes. She squinted against the sting of the smoke, which curled up from her cigarette, and she said in a different tone, "Honey? Somebody's trying to get in touch with you. Somebody needs your help. Somebody's calling . . ."

Ann's blood froze, and she yanked her hand away. Sister Angela looked startled. Lily stopped in the midst of applying her nail polish and, brush poised in midair, rested her eyes heavily on Ann, who stared back as something occurred to her. The little Gypsy with the scarfs and shawls in her dream . . . Could it be Lily? Lily with her earrings and her Gypsy mother? Lily and her Gift? Lily who always watched her in school? Lily who had helped her? Lily . . .

"Go on, Mom," Lily said, her eyes never leaving Ann's face.

"Not if she don't want me to," Sister Angela said. Then she smiled and shrugged. "Anyway, it's gone. I can't see no more. Is there something wrong, honey?" Her black eyes looked kindly into Ann's.

Ann's heart pounded in her ears. "No . . . It's just that I've been having a nightmare about someone calling me and . . ."

Lily and her mother did not seem surprised by the coincidence.

"Honey, what you are calling a nightmare," Sister Angela said in a soothing voice, "is just a message, and you shouldn't be afraid of no message. Probably somebody just wants to talk to you. Maybe it's you, making up the dream because you want to tell yourself something. Maybe it's someone from beyond. You see, honey, we walk around in one world, but there's another world. Dreams are just a door to that other world. It's nothing to be afraid of."

Ann was not reassured. She stared into her lap and gathered her courage.

"Lily?" She looked intently at her new friend. "Is it you?"

Lily met her eyes for a moment before answering calmly, "No, it's not me."

"It's either you trying to tell yourself something, honey," Sister Angela said firmly, "or it's someone from the other side."

"The . . . other side?" Ann felt weak and a little dizzy.

"Tell me, honey, do you know anybody who died?" Sister Angela leaned forward interestedly.

That was too much. Ann stood up. The sweet, spicy smell of the room was becoming overpowering.

"No," she said, "I don't know anyone . . . like

that. I have to go home now. Thank you for everything. I really have to go home." She moved toward the door.

"Good-bye now," Sister Angela called after her. "You come back whenever you want, and don't you worry about nothing."

Lily did not accompany Ann to the door; she simply watched her leave, her dark eyes grave and troubled.

Ann flew down the steps and burst gratefully out into the noise and brilliant sunlight of the street.

"Ann, where on earth have you been? I've been worried," Mother said as soon as Ann got home.

"I went to a friend's house after school," Ann said, slamming her bookbag forcefully against the wall.

"Don't do that! Go and pick it up immediately," Mother said angrily.

Ann grumpily obeyed.

"I'm happy to hear that you've made a friend, but it was very inconsiderate of you not to call. I have enough to worry about with these publishing people coming for dinner tonight."

After what she had been through, Ann could think of nothing more trivial than some people coming over for dinner.

"I'm sorry I didn't call," Ann said, adding to

herself, I had much more important things to think about. She wanted to go up to her room and consider in private everything Sister Angela had said.

"Well, try not to forget again. Now, Isabelle is down at the park playing with friends. I want you to run down there and walk her home."

Ann groaned.

"It's getting late, and she's too young to walk all that way alone."

"If she's too young to walk home, she's too young to play in the park in the first place," Ann growled.

"Don't be silly, Ann."

There was nothing that stung Ann more than being called silly.

"I'm surprised you mind doing a simple thing like this," her mother continued. "I'd go myself if I didn't have so much to do."

Ann left, slamming the door. This was too unfair. Here I am, she thought bitterly, haunted by some ghost, and I have to go pick up my stupid sister because my mother is having a stupid dinner party for her stupid friends. The whole thing's incredibly stupid!

Isabelle was playing alone on the tall swings.

"Come on," Ann said shortly. "It's time to go home."

"I don't want to go home."

"You have to. Hurry up."

"I don't *want* to go home!"

"Isabelle?"

"I'm not going home unless you give me a push first."

Give her a push? I'll give her a push all right, Ann thought furiously. She ran again and again under the swing, pushing it higher and higher until the chain began to buckle. Isabelle screamed for Ann to stop, but she would not. Isabelle's shrieks began to attract disapproving stares from mothers in the park.

"Leave that poor girl alone!" one woman snapped. "What a horrid little thing you are!"

Blushing with fury and shame, Ann stopped the swing, grabbed Isabelle's hand, and ran at top speed across the park.

"Stop!" Isabelle gasped through her tears. "You're going too fast!"

Ann did not slow down. She pulled the wailing girl all the way home and flung her into the living room, where Isabelle flopped herself dramatically on the floor at her mother's feet. Ann ran up to her room to the sound of Isabelle's sobbing accusations.

Minutes later the door was flung open by her extremely angry mother.

"Ann, I cannot understand why you are so unkind to Isabelle. This has been going on for years now, and I'd really hoped that you would grow out of it, but you haven't. When are you going to understand that she is a sweet little girl and not your mortal enemy? I'm tired of this. You ought to know better."

Mother paused expectantly, but Ann stared grimly at the floor.

"I can't see any reason for your behavior, Ann. You're a very intelligent girl. You're a year ahead in school. I expect more from you. Because you're older, Isabelle respects you and looks up to you. And that's why it hurts her so much when you're cruel. Don't you see that?"

Ann exploded. "I don't want to be intelligent! I don't want to be a year ahead in school! Why do I have to be older? It isn't fair!"

Mother ignored Ann's outburst. "You must come down and apologize. I'll be very angry if you don't."

"But —"

"Right now!"

Mother marched Ann down to the kitchen. Isabelle was wearing an apron and helping to prepare for the party by putting toothpicks in olives and mushrooms. She turned her large, injured eyes to Ann, who thought it was just like Isabelle to have the only fun job of a dinner party. If I were helping too, I would have to set the table or do some other dull job. It just isn't fair to give the fun job to one sister because she's too incompetent to do any of the harder jobs. Ann looked up at her mother, leaning against the wall, arms crossed, waiting not too patiently.

"I'm sorry," Ann muttered between clenched teeth without looking Isabelle in the eye.

"That's all right, Annie," Isabelle said in an infuriatingly sweet voice. "The lady in the park said you were horrid, but you're not. Not really. I forgive you."

This was too much. "I'm sorry," Ann hissed. "I'm sorry you are such a slow runner! I'm sorry you don't know how to walk back from the stupid park by yourself!" She turned to her mother. "And I'm sorry you have such a terrible older daughter! I'm sorry! I'm sorry!"

Ann ran back up the stairs, bursting into tears as she slammed her door shut. She spent the rest of the evening in exile, listening to the gales of laughter from the guests downstairs. She knew that Isabelle was helping to serve the meal and saying cute things and being told what a lovely little girl she was. She always showed off when guests came over. Sometimes she even performed ridiculous little dances, and everyone always thought she was adorable.

Forced to remain in her cold garret while the family was entertaining guests because they were all ashamed of her, plagued by ghosts all night long, little Ann tried to accept her position as the unwanted child with a cheerful . . .

Eventually she fell into a hot, troubled sleep.

CHAPTER EIGHT

On the Job

*T*he day after the dinner party, Mother, Father, and Isabelle treated Ann with their usual cheer and friendliness, but Ann continued to sulk. Knowing that she had behaved badly made her angry with herself, and that anger spilled over to include those around her. To her earlier cry of "Why do I have to be older?" was added the equally unanswerable question, "Why do I always have to be the one who's wrong?" In a strange way, she resented the fact that her punishment had not been more severe and lasting. If only they had locked me in my room for three days without food or water, she thought, we would be even. As it was, she felt doomed to be forever the terrible sister, with no chance of penance and punishment that would free her of guilt.

As the days passed, however, Ann slowly became cheerful again, almost against her will. It is very difficult to keep up a good strong pout for days on end. She decided to make amends by being nice to Isabelle from then on. In time, they would all say, "Isn't Ann a wonderful sister? What a change has come over her!" That was a pleasant thought, and Ann entertained herself for days with stories of how she would, at great personal risk, rescue Isabelle from various dangers: waterfalls, bullies in the park, wolves in the closet, and the like.

Thus it was that Ann greeted the next Saturday morning with high spirits, resolved to become a better person in every way. She got out of bed and sat right down at her desk to get the weekend's homework out of the way first thing under the gaze of Pecony Bear, who still sat on her desk, surveying the work of the new Ann with approval. She felt so righteous and capable that her pencil fairly flew, and she polished it all off in under an hour. Sometimes doing homework was quite satisfying, especially when there wasn't too much and it wasn't put off until the dreaded Sunday night. I'm such a good student, Ann admitted to herself after she drew a straight line with her ruler under the last math problem.

The homework neatly set aside, she turned to the task of giving her room a vigorous cleaning. She made the bed perfectly, folded all her clothes and stacked them in the wardrobe, and shook her small rug. Shaking the rug! Ann was almost giddy

with the industriousness of it all. She surveyed
the room critically to see what else she could do.
A-ha, the sink! Ann scrubbed the sink until it
gleamed.

*Yes, Ann was clean. From an early age she showed
that no dirt was going to get past her! She did the work
of three women, and always with a smile. Even the
neighbors noticed it. "That girl is clean!" they often
said. "And such a good student!" They usually added,
"And a magnificent sister, too."*

I must clean my room like this every day, Ann
thought. And maybe the whole house. If I got up
earlier, I could do three rooms before school and
the rest after I got home. That would really make
Mother happy, and she'd have more time to de-
vote to Isabelle.

And then, if the neighbors had a really big mess,
they would call on me. Little Ann's Cleaning, Inc.:
"Ann Gets the Job Done." Weekends, I could do
the whole block; then during the summer vaca-
tion I could —

She was suddenly struck with a vision of a bucket
and sponge sitting unused on top of other unused things. THE PILE!

Bravely, she pushed the thought aside. This
time it would be different. Ann stood back to ad-
mire the sink. Now, what else? She could always
wash the window, but . . . Since the nightmares
had started, she had avoided the window end of

her room. Although she had been more occupied with the Isabelle problem lately, she had not forgotten Sister Angela's words: "the other side." No, no, she wouldn't think about it now. Then, too, she was feeling rather hungry.

It is very important for a world-famous cleaner to keep her strength up by eating regularly. "I could never have done it without food," Ann told the reporters.

When she entered the kitchen, Ann found Father sitting at the table, drinking coffee. "Ann, honey," he said, "I have some work to catch up on at the office this morning. Would you like to come along?"

"Oh, yes!" Ann loved going to work with her father.

"Fine. Why don't you run and find Isabelle and ask her if she'd like to come along too?"

Isabelle? Isabelle come too? What would be the fun in that? The best part of going to Father's office was being alone with him.

"I don't think Isabelle can come. I heard her say she was going over to Hilary's this morning," Ann said, knowing full well she was lying. Old habits died hard.

"All right. It'll just be the two of us then," Father said.

That's more like it, Ann thought gleefully. The two set off hand in hand across the park toward the university. On the way, Ann told her father about her way of walking to school by stepping on all the cracks, even bricks. Father laughed and said he had done the same thing as a boy, only he had avoided all the cracks. Ann was pleased to discover this bond between them. It was hard to imagine Father as a boy, though. The best she could come up with was a tiny version of a grown man, wearing short pants and a cap. Then she tried to picture herself as a grownup. That was just as difficult. There are some things a person just cannot know, she decided comfortably.

Father's building looked just as it should: square, stone, and important. They walked down empty, echoing halls, clanged up curving metal staircases, and stopped in front of his office door. Ann eyed her father's big bunch of keys enviously.

Work, she thought. This is Work. When you grow up, you get a job and an office, and some Saturday mornings you just have to go there and catch up. It's not always easy, but it has to be done. Fortunately, you have your big bunch of keys. Of course, what Mother did was Work too, but it didn't seem nearly as much fun. Being a writer seemed to Ann suspiciously like one big, fat, life-long homework assignment, and, what's more, writers had to have all those rotten dinner parties. There were very few keys involved and no large buildings.

The office looked just as she remembered it. A

large desk covered with papers stood in the middle of the room. Father sat behind the desk in a swivel chair that creaked as he spun around, moving from desk to typewriter to filing cabinet. This was a place where things got done! Ann could see that. A faint odor of cigarette smoke hung in the air. Near the desk was a large gray wastebasket surrounded by balled-up pieces of paper that hadn't quite made it in. *When the job's got to be done, you don't always have time to aim.* On a shelf next to a coffee machine were paper cups, plastic spoons, and a box of sugar cubes. For as long as she could remember, Ann had eaten one of those sugar cubes each time she came to the office. She didn't really like the taste, but it was a tradition. She popped one into her mouth now and crunched down happily on the grainy sweetness.

Now Father was talking on the telephone. It was a complicated work phone with plenty of buttons that lit up. When the phone rang, you pushed the button that flashed. That way you could talk to more than one person at a time — and when you are really working you sometimes have to, Ann knew.

Ann left the office to adventure down the lonely halls. Her shoes made a sharp, businesslike clicking against the tile floors. When I grow up, she thought, I'll have an office just like this. It'll say on the door: Ann's Office. I'll have a coffee machine and a typewriter and lots of papers to sort and throw away. People will call me all day long, and those buttons will flash like mad.

There's one thing you could be sure of: Ann always pushed the right button on her phone, no matter how many of them were flashing. It was a kind of gift she had.

And sometimes I'll have to walk along the halls the way I'm doing now in order to inspect. *To inspect.* That sounded good.

It was time for Ann to inspect. It was hard work, but somebody had to do it. Yes, everything seemed to be in order. Some doors were open — good, good — so you could peek in. And some doors were shut — good, good — just as they should be, Ann was satisfied to note. She had to keep her eye on things.

She passed an open door where two men were talking. They stopped when they saw her.

"May I help you?" one of them asked.

Ann felt embarrassed. "My father works here," she stammered.

"Okay. Well, little lady, you just keep an eye on things for us here." The two men laughed.

Ann's cheeks burned. How had they guessed? Why did people try to wreck every one of her games? Refusing to let this one be destroyed, she went back to her father's office and found it empty. She followed the sound of his voice and saw that he was with another man in a room filled with machines. They were tinkering with one of them.

"It seems to be jammed," Father said. "I wish these people would take better care of the hardware."

Hardware . . . Ann could see it now . . .

Working Woman Ann was in her office, busy with typing and phoning when suddenly Hank, her assistant, burst in.

"The hardware!" he shouted. "It's out of control!"

Ann rushed into the equipment room. Yes, it looked bad. Ann ran an experienced eye over the machines. "They seem to be jammed," she said thoughtfully. "The modulator is revving too high!"

"Do something fast, Ann. We've only got three minutes before the quasar exterminates!" Hank rasped, panicked.

"Give me a monkey wrench," Ann said coolly.

"Two minutes left!" Hank gasped. "We're losing air pressure!"

Ann worked quickly and efficiently with the wrench, tightening the levers and severing the valves.

"It's our only chance, Hank," she said with surprising calm. "Let's hope it works."

"The building's going to blow!" Hank screamed.

After a few more deft adjustments with the wrench, the needle on the Danger Meter returned to Safe. Hank slumped to the floor, unconscious. Ann pocketed the trusty wrench and returned to her office. At times like these, you just have to keep a clear head and —

"Ann," Father's voice cut in. "Ann? I think we've got everything set here. Would you like to help me for a little while? I have some work you could do."

The work consisted of taking one sheet of paper from each of three piles, stapling them together in the right order, and laying the stapled pages in stacks of fifteen. Ann worked carefully, lining the corners up just right and then — *bang!* — pounding in a shiny staple. *The secret documents had to be finished that night or the cause would be lost.* Ann lost count in one stack and had to start over. She picked up the papers, and they slipped to the floor. In the process of gathering them up, Ann ripped two. She couldn't find any tape to repair them, so she quietly slipped them under the third pile. Progress was slow, and the repetition was numbing to her imagination. *One thing you could say about this job of working on Secret Documents: It was* . . . And the truth hit her. *Dull!* This job was endless and dull!

"I've finished my work, Ann," Father said. "Let's get something to drink and go home. Someone else can finish those on Monday."

Ann looked up gratefully. In my office, she decided, there won't be much stapling. Perhaps none at all.

Near Father's office was a shiny gray diner, the perfect place to go for a drink after work.

The steam rose slowly from Father's cup of coffee. Ann wished she liked the taste of coffee, because it was the right thing to have after a hard day at work. Instead she sipped her orange juice, which was all wrong but tasted better. The diner was half empty and there were several free tables, but father and daughter sat at the counter. This was as it should be. Tables were for when the whole family went out. Counters were for special private outings.

This seemed as good a time as any to ask the question that had been bothering her ever since her visit to Lily's house and Sister Angela.

"Father, do I know anybody who died?"

Father looked surprised. "I don't think so. Why do you ask?"

"I was just wondering," Ann said vaguely. She didn't want to mention Sister Angela because all that would take too much explaining. Besides, her father might not approve.

"No, I don't think so," Father repeated and began to read a newspaper someone had abandoned. But Ann could not allow the matter to rest there.

"Nobody at all? No friend I had when I was little? A neighbor, maybe?"

"No one I can think of, darling."

"Well, did anybody in the family die? A relative or something?"

"Well, dear . . ." Father spoke slowly and rather reluctantly. "Since you ask, there was one death in our family, but you never knew that person."

"Who was it?"

"When your mother and I had been married for two years, we had a baby who died after only a few days. The baby was born too soon and wasn't strong enough to live. Then, a year later, we had you."

Ann was silent for a long moment. "Was it a girl?" she asked softly.

"Yes."

Ann was shaken. A girl. From the other side. Someone Ann ought to recognize . . . Her sister! Ann struggled to comprehend this new and perplexing idea.

"You mean, if she hadn't died, I wouldn't be the oldest?"

"That's right."

"So maybe you wouldn't have had Isabelle at all? There would only have been two of us, and I would have been the youngest?"

"It's hard to say, darling. I'd hate to imagine the family without Isabelle. Maybe we would have had three little girls."

"And I would have been in the middle?"

"In that case, yes."

All this was very hard to grasp. Ann had always considered her role as first-born child, with all its advantages and disadvantages, to be exclusively hers. That was who and what she was: the first girl in the family. And now the knowledge that she might not have been the first frightened her with an overwhelming sense of how haphazard the world is. If the first girl hadn't died, *she* would have been Ann. Then a chilling thought occurred to her. Would I have been . . . Isabelle? Me? *I* would have been Isabelle? Could personality and character be based only on the order in which children were born?

Ann's mind reeled.

As they walked home, another thought struck her.

"Do you and Mother feel sad about her?"

"At the time we did, darling, of course. And still a little now. But, much more than that, we feel very happy and lucky to have the two intelligent, beautiful daughters we have."

He smiled and took Ann's hand. When they reached the house, he gave her a hug and kiss.

"I'd like to wait a few years before telling Isabelle about this," he said. "I wouldn't like her to learn something that might upset her when she's still too young to understand."

Ann agreed readily. In fact, she wasn't entirely sure that she was old enough to understand it herself. But one thing seemed clear. The little Gypsy in her dreams was her sister, a sister calling out to her. Ann thought of fairy tales about people who were under enchantments. Maybe her sister was under a spell and needed help, and only Ann could free her.

She considered her next step seriously. After all, Sister Angela had told her that no one in a dream could hurt her. Bravely, Ann decided that when she had her next dream, she would do whatever the little Gypsy asked.

CHAPTER NINE

Ann Entertains

*I*n science class on Monday morning, Mrs. Weed announced that they were going to begin a new project. The students were to divide into groups of two, collect various kinds of plants, pin them to a board, label them, and finally present their collections to the rest of the class together with oral reports about where the plants grew, how much sun and water they required, what uses they had, and other interesting information. Ann sighed deeply. Among the things she disliked most were science, oral reports, and teamwork. She was very disappointed that Mrs. Weed had come up with something that combined all three.

There was an excited murmur when Mrs. Weed mentioned the groups of two, and the class paired off quickly into the usual best friends. Ann found both Lily and Fernando looking at her hopefully. First she hadn't had any friends, and now she had too many. It was difficult being popular. She couldn't choose between them, so she kept her head down and waited.

After the bustle had subsided, Mrs. Weed said, "Now raise your hands, whoever is left over." Usually Ann had been the only one left over, and when teachers assigned her to a team of friends, they would groan and sigh.

Timidly, Ann, Lily, and Fernando put their hands up. What good luck!

"May the three of us work together?" Ann asked.

"Well, all right," Mrs. Weed said. "But I'll expect an especially good project from your group since there are three of you."

Ann beamed at her friends.

At the beginning of recess, Ann and Lily met and looked around the playground. One group of girls was playing four-square; another was jumping rope; and the third, which consisted of the dullest and most popular girls in the class, was sitting in a circle, singing songs and rocking to and fro. Marie Sternberg would certainly have chosen that last group, but Ann and Lily decided to jump rope, where the girls twirling the rope were chanting:

Cin-der-el-la dressed in yel-la
Went upstairs to kiss her fel-la

Made a mistake and kissed a snake
How many doctors did it take?
One . . . Two . . . Three . . . Four . . .

Pudgy Beth was skipping. She usually didn't last longer than seven or eight. Suddenly, with a shout, Fernando bounded in and began jumping alongside Beth. These raids on the jump rope were something Fernando did only occasionally, when he was in an especially good mood. Beth rushed out from under the rope and began to whine that her turn had been ruined. Fernando was not only the fastest runner in the class, he was also the best rope jumper. Soon the girls twirling the rope began to complain that their arms were getting tired, and Lily and Ann took over as Fernando laughed and jumped on tirelessly. The boys on the other side of the playground saw him and ran to join in. Mike Dunk arrived, puffing and bawling, "My turn! My turn!"

Ann scowled. Fernando's visits to the jump rope were always welcome, but Mike Dunk's were a different matter altogether. Mike stopped the rope with his hand. "My turn!"

Fernando never fought with the other boys, so he stood aside, smiling, as Ann considered a plan.

"Lily," she said brightly, "let's twirl the rope for Mike."

Lily smiled back knowingly. When Mike had reached the count of ten, Ann nodded to Lily, and the two began to twirl the rope at slightly different speeds. Without being noticeable to onlookers, it gave the rope enough of a torque to make it very difficult to jump. As expected, Mike's legs soon got entangled.

"You're cheating!" he yelled at Ann.

"Next," she called cheerfully.

"It's just a stupid girls' game," Mike growled as he went to rejoin the boys playing kickball.

Through this subtle method, Ann and Lily quickly discouraged all the jumpers but Fernando, who got as far as fifty before he volunteered to twirl for a while. Then he and Ann twirled the rope for Lily, and afterward they walked around together and chatted about the science project. Ann was pleased that her two friends got along so well, and she felt the pleasure of an experienced hostess whose dinner party is running smoothly. When the bell rang to go back in, Ann had not yet had a turn at the jump rope, but she reasoned that one must always make sacrifices for friends.

That afternoon Ann took Lily home with her. She was proud to show her mother that she had made a friend at last, but she was a little nervous about how to entertain her guest. No one at Ann's house could do anything interesting, like tell fortunes, and she feared that Lily would find her house rather flat and dull. There was no orange or purple to be seen anywhere. Mother made tea, as she had promised, and served it to the girls quite fancily in the living room, with the good cups and both sandwiches and slices of cake. She even offered Lily the use of the telephone to tell her mother she would be late, but Lily shrugged and said that it wasn't necessary. Her mother trusted her. Ann couldn't help throwing a look of satisfaction toward her mother.

Later, up in Ann's garret room, Lily asked as she looked thoughtfully out the dormer window, "Do you still have those dreams?"

The flat tone of Lily's voice made Ann uncomfortable. "Oh, I haven't had one for a long time." Then she decided to tell Lily about her sister who had died. ". . . so I decided to do what she wants me to the next time I have the dream. Do you think that's a good idea?" she asked anxiously.

"Yes," Lily said. "If she's calling you, it's for a reason. You should feel privileged that she chooses to communicate with you. Who knows? Maybe you have the gift, too!"

Ann was thrilled. The Gift! She would never have thought about that by herself. She could see why people liked having friends.

Down in the kitchen, Ann and Lily found Isabelle busy making cookies. She was wearing an apron and standing on a chair at the counter, stirring batter in a large bowl and looking relentlessly cute. Sticky pans and spoons were piled high on every available surface, and the prints of Isabelle's bare feet were clearly visible in the dusting of flour covering the floor.

"Hi, Annie. Hello . . . Do you want to help me make cookies? I could show you how. It's really fun."

Making cookies was one of life's pleasures, and if Ann had been alone, she would have enjoyed helping Isabelle. But she was afraid it would sound dull and babyish to Lily, a girl who painted her nails and wore hoop earrings. Besides, it's almost a duty to scorn one's younger siblings and all their silly doings when one has a friend over.

"No, we don't want to make any stupid cookies," Ann said rudely.

Isabelle looked offended and ran out of the kitchen to ask her mother about the next step. Then Ann got a wonderful idea. Even better than just scorning the cookies, she could sabotage them! That way she could really show Lily how insignificant Isabelle was and how grown up they were by comparison.

"Watch, Lily," she whispered. She grabbed the salt box and poured a huge quantity into the bowl. Then she mixed it well so that the batter looked exactly as it had before. Ann was rewarded by a laugh from Lily, but almost immediately her heart fell as she remembered her plans to be the perfect older sister.

Sisterhood: one more thing for THE PILE.

Still, when the visit came to an end, Ann was satisfied with her afternoon. As she returned from walking Lily to the corner, she hummed to herself contentedly.

Ann, the famous international hostess, began early in life to entertain friends at her home, and her tea parties soon became the envy of the neighborhood. Everyone clamored for invitations, perhaps because they knew she had . . . the Gift!

After dinner, Isabelle came out of the kitchen beaming with the plate of cookies she had made.

"And for dessert," Mother announced proudly, "we have a special surprise. Isabelle made these all by herself."

Well, almost, Ann thought.

"Mommy put them in the oven for me and took them out," Isabelle admitted, not wanting to claim more than her share of the credit. She passed them around, smiling with anticipation. Everyone tasted them. Ann's own bite was rather small.

There was a moment of embarrassed silence.

Isabelle's face wrinkled up. "They're horrible!" she wailed.

"Honey," Mother said gently, "I think you made a mistake with the salt and the sugar. Did you use the red canister or the blue one?"

"The red one!" Isabelle said, sobbing. "I know I didn't make a mistake. I tasted the sugar to make sure before I put it in!"

The flicker of a glance Mother directed to Ann made her ears grow warm.

"I think they're good," Ann said quickly, for lack of anything else to say.

"Do you really, Ann?" Mother asked evenly.

"In a way. Sort of." Ann retreated.

"You know, darling," Father said, pulling Isabelle onto his lap, "it's a very easy mistake to make on your first batch of cookies. In fact, it's almost a tradition."

"Really?" Isabelle asked moistly.

"Indeed, yes. Some of the best chefs in the world have confused salt and sugar, and they were grown men working in fancy restaurants."

Isabelle sniffed and stopped crying.

"And you can imagine the faces of the people who bit into salty éclairs and sipped sweet fish soup!"

Isabelle gave a watery smile.

"I'll tell you what," Mother said. "Since Ann thinks your cookies are so good . . ."

Oh no! Ann thought, imagining herself having to choke down all those salty cookies.

". . . perhaps she could —"

"I know," Ann said quickly. "I'll help you next time, Isabelle, and they'll be delicious. You'll see."

"Thanks, Annie," Isabelle said with a smile.

"Oh, that's all right," Ann said sweetly. But she avoided her mother's eyes.

"Isabelle," Mother suggested, "I think you've been the innocent victim of . . . an unfortunate mistake. I'd like to make it up to you somehow. How about just you and me getting all dressed up one day after school and going to the Copley for an elegant tea?"

"Oh, goody," Isabelle shouted, her face radiant with happiness, although her cheeks were still damp with tears.

A slight nod from Mother told Ann that the matter would remain between them and would go no further. She felt a stab of remorse for the dirty trick she had played on her sister, but in a way it was Isabelle's own fault. If she weren't so easy to fool, it wouldn't happen. And if she weren't so cute and bubbling with happiness all the time, it wouldn't be such a pleasure to burst her balloon of joy. But Ann couldn't convince herself that it was really Isabelle's fault for being so vulnerable and trusting. Deep down she knew that she was a mean, mean older sister. Then something occurred to her. If the dream sister had lived, she thought, I would be a middle sister or a younger sister. Maybe I'm not any good at being an older sister because I wasn't meant to be one. Maybe it isn't my fault at all. Maybe it's just that . . . But she couldn't find any consolation in these excuses. She was too intelligent and logical to fool herself. The simple fact was, she was a horrid sister.

"Don't you recognize me?" The voice was soft and sad, as though it was on the verge of giving up hope. The tone of the dream was changing. Even the wind blew less violently, and the carnival music had a minor key and sounded as if it were coming from miles away.

Ann strode bravely to the window and looked down at the Gypsy standing below. Her face was concealed in the folds of her shawl, which was somehow not stirred by the wind that blew so strongly into Ann's face. Suddenly, as it had before, the wind changed direction, pushing Ann against the window, and she clung fearfully to the sill.

"Ann . . . Ann . . ." The voice beckoned to her.

This is my sister who needs me, Ann thought. I can't abandon her. With great effort, she forced herself to release her grip on the sill. The strong suction lifted her as though she were weightless and drew her through the window. Oddly, there was no crash, no sharp edges of broken glass. The pane transformed itself into a thin, transparent waterfall of mist. After passing through it, Ann felt nothing more than a few drops of dew clinging to her nightgown.

The wind carried her swiftly at first, then more and more gently forward and down. After the initial fright of being lifted off her feet, Ann quite enjoyed the descent. It was a bit like a roller coaster, only in reverse. She started out fast and finished slowly. As she floated toward the fair, the music grew louder and the lights brighter. Then, suddenly, she felt the rough, dry grass under her bare feet.

Ann looked around in bewilderment. From gaily painted, glaringly lit booths on either side, carnival workers with masklike faces leaned over their counters and shouted down at her, their faces looming large.

"Step up, little lady. Three balls for a quarter. A winner every time! You wanna be a winner, don't you, little lady? You wanna be a success, don't you?"

"Here you go, girlie-girl. Here's your last chance to be a famous sharpshooter! Hit three ducks and this fuzzy little Pecony Bear is yours! Try your skill!"

"Figure out the answer, and you win the game!

Here's a test for the smart people! Hey there, tiny tot, you're one of the smart people, aren't you? Figure out the answer, and you win!"

Through all the babel and confusion, Ann heard the distant but clear voice: "Ann? Ann?"

There, next to the candied apple stand, stood the little Gypsy. A large scarf over her head made it impossible for Ann to see her face. As she ran toward the figure, Ann collided with a huge man rushing in the opposite direction and was knocked down.

"Watch where you're going, kid," the huge man said gruffly. "If you wanna get somewhere in life, you got to watch where you're going!"

By the time Ann had picked herself up, the Gypsy had disappeared into the mass of people, all of whom had their faces covered with scarves and shawls. Ann pressed on, squirming through the throng, which moved mechanically forward, all at the same regular pace, none of them seeming to notice her presence. The Gypsy's voice had sounded so pathetic and helpless. Ann had to do something to help her sister, but she didn't know what. She struggled to free herself from the crowd of faceless people, all laughing loudly behind their scarves, and her apprehension grew until she heard her name called again, this time from the top of the ferris wheel. She rushed to its base and peered into each car as it circled down. She recognized students and teachers from school, but the Gypsy wasn't there.

Didn't the Gypsy want Ann to catch up with her? Was she just teasing her? Or was someone preventing them from meeting?

Out of the corner of her eye, Ann saw the Gypsy girl flit past, little more than a flash of color. She ran as fast as she could after the fleeing form, dodging the people trudging numbly in her path. As she ran, the wind flowed over her body. Then it became stronger and swirled around her, picking her up and carrying her far above the carnival, back through the water window and into her bed. When Ann felt the blankets tucked around her, she woke up.

She struggled to stay awake and mull over her adventure and its meaning, but she was overcome by a heavy, irresistible sleepiness.

CHAPTER TEN

Exiled

*T*he next morning Ann awoke with a feeling of expectant excitement. Her dream no longer frightened her. Instead, she wished desperately to return to the carnival, because she was sure if she ran just a little faster the next time and kept a little sharper lookout, she would catch the Gypsy. And if I don't catch her next time, Ann thought, then I'll keep trying until I do. Ann knew from her experience in reading fairy tales that the only way to break an enchantment was to persevere loyally.

But what should Ann say when she finally caught up with her dream sister? How does one address a dead sister one has never met? Ann practiced conversations out loud in her room.

"Hello. I'm happy to meet you." No, that sounded too formal and stiff, even though it was true.

"Hi. My name is Ann. What's yours?" This

greeting had two problems. First, the girl already knew Ann's name, and second, since she had died so soon after birth, there was a good possibility she didn't have a name. It wouldn't do to rub it in.

"What do you want of me?" No, no. That was too theatrical.

As Ann pondered, she had the delicious feeling of possessing a very special and fascinating problem. Most children only read about things like this, she thought happily, but it's really happening to me. Now that the dreams had become a source of pride, Ann was bursting to talk about them. She considered telling Lily about the latest episode but decided against it, fearing that talking about it might somehow break the spell and ruin her chances of returning to the carnival.

It's so difficult to know what is right and what is wrong in a magical situation. Ann decided not to risk it, so she did the second best thing: she daydreamed a story about it.

From an early age, the doors of the spirit world had been open to little Ann. Other times, other places, other lives, held no secrets for her. In fact, she became world famous for having . . . the Gift . . .

Eager to return to the dream, Ann was impatient for the day to end so she could go to sleep. But it dragged on and on. Isabelle's game of pirates was louder and messier than usual. She had draped sheets all over her room for sails again, and her shouts of "Ahoy, Mate! Ahoy, Mate!" were irritating beyond belief. Tempted to explain how ridiculous it was to pretend a bed was a ship on the high seas, Ann stepped into Isabelle's littered room.

"Ahoy, Mate!" Isabelle cried.

"Really, Isabelle, that game is too . . ." But Ann remembered her vow to be kinder to her sister, so she only shook her head sadly, rolled her eyes, and left.

Mother was having one of her serious work days when she needed peace and quiet, sometimes pounding on her typewriter, sometimes pacing and talking out loud in her study behind a gently but firmly closed door.

And Father was doing work around the house, wandering distractedly into the kitchen from time to time, muttering something about his lost hammer.

Much earlier than usual, in fact before the evening sky visible through her window had darkened into full night, Ann dove into bed. She tried to fall asleep immediately, but sleep would not come. Several times she got out of bed and looked down from her window, but she saw only her own back yard, peaceful, silent, and ordinary. Hours later she fell asleep, only to awake the next morn-

ing from a disappointingly normal, uneventful
rest.

Several days dragged on in this way: Ann going
to bed eagerly, only to wake up disappointed. It
occurred to her that this dream might be one of
those things that only happen when you're not
thinking about them. Many things are like that.
Ann had noticed that, for example, she never got
a letter in the mail on days when she was bored
and really wanted one. Letters usually arrived on
days that were already so good and full of inter-
est that mail was almost wasted. Then there was
the case of the dim star that you could only see
when you looked away from it and which disappeared when you looked directly at it. Of course,
Ann realized, the dim star wasn't really the same
sort of thing as the awaited letter never arriving,
but there were similarities of a spiritual sort.
Taking all this thinking into consideration, Ann
developed a new strategy. She concentrated on
not thinking about the dream, hoping to trick it
into recurring. She lay in bed thinking loudly and
with careful mental diction, "Here I am, just
thinking about school and nothing else. School.
School. School. Not dreams at all —" Oops! That
last part just slipped out. "No, no! I'm just thinking about school and teachers and recess and
projects, and perhaps I'll just think of what to say

to her when I see her. Will she run away from me again and make me chase . . ."

Ann gave up. It was impossible to keep the dream out of her thoughts, and she knew that the dream could hear everything in her head. It was no use.

Under the weight of this new frustration, Ann's resolve to treat her sister more kindly crumbled. As always when Ann was upset about something, Isabelle took the brunt, and her actions seemed more maddening than usual. She ruined Ann's favorite fairy tale book (the one with the illustrations that had determined for Ann forever the idea of how a proper princess — and castle, and ogre, and chest of treasure — looked) by leaving it outside in the rain overnight. And, worst of all, Isabelle forced poor Pecony Bear to play with that dull Segeener for an entire afternoon until Ann found out and rescued him. In retaliation, Ann teased, threatened, bullied, and frightened her little sister during the next several days until Isabelle was driven to complaining to Mother.

Mother was beyond anger. She sat Ann down and spoke to her in that flat, neutral voice that was much more frightening than her angry one.

"Ann, I don't know what to do. I thought that giving you your own room would lessen the tension between the two of you, but that doesn't seem to be the case. You continue to mistreat your sister. There's no excuse for the shameless way you ruined her cookies, for example. I honestly don't know what to do with you. Do you have any suggestions?"

Ann didn't. She felt guilty and resentful and misunderstood. It's too much, she thought, to make a girl worry about things in two different worlds at once. I'm trying to help one sister, and everyone keeps bothering me about the other one.

"I simply don't understand," Mother continued. "When I was your age, I was too involved with other things to waste time fighting with my sisters. I read everything I could find, and when I wasn't reading, I was writing little stories of my own. Maybe that's your problem: maybe you have too much spare time. I know your schoolwork isn't interesting or challenging enough to keep your mind occupied. Have you ever thought of taking up a hobby? Painting, or sewing, or playing an instrument —"

If only you knew, Ann thought bitterly.

"— or dancing, or learning French. *Anything.* You know your father and I would be happy to help you. Please give it some serious thought. In the meantime, tell me this. What exactly is it that Isabelle does to annoy you so?"

Ann wasn't able to offer particulars that didn't seem awfully trivial or nitpicking. It was more a matter of total effect than of individual acts of messiness or cuteness or dumbness. It was one of those things that if you didn't already understand, you never would. But she promised (again) to try to be loving to her sister or, at the very least, to be civil (if possible).

As the days passed, Ann found herself having to accept the possibility that the spell was broken and that the dream would never return. It had been well over a week since the last one, after all. Maybe one chance to catch the Gypsy and discover her message was all she would be given. It looked as though she was bound to the earth forever, never again to float freely from the window.

In addition to all her other troubles, Ann had no patience for irritations in school, but the due date for the science project was drawing near, and every day more of her classmates came in with plants to classify and pin to their boards. Ann noticed with particular annoyance that Patty's group had nearly finished. Their plants were covered with clear plastic and attached to pieces of brightly colored construction paper, and the margins were decorated with perfect little drawings of butterflies, mushrooms, and bluebirds. Ann shuddered at the unscientific cuteness of it all.

Lily and Fernando were hard at work as well, and they seemed to be enjoying the project. For her part, Ann couldn't think of anything dumber than picking weeds and looking up their names in a book. She didn't like to appear to be shirking her part of the work, so she told her friends that she was doing hers at home.

Thursday afternoon, sitting dejectedly on the edge of her bed, Ann reviewed the situation grimly. The next day was Friday, and the project was due Monday, so she really should bring a few plants to school to show Lily and Fernando that she wasn't lazy or incompetent. That meant gathering them right away. But she wasn't in the mood. She took her marbles out of a wooden box in the wardrobe and spilled them listlessly onto the floor. Ann didn't play with marbles in the conventional way. She played school with them. Once a rude person had pointed out that this was the wrong thing to do with marbles, and she had been quite indignant because, in fact, playing school was a very fun thing to do with them, whereas knocking one against the other in an effort to capture them was rather like a silly, boyish war game. The larger marbles were teachers and the largest of all was the principal. The smaller ones were the students, and Ann divided them into classes according to color: red, blue, green, and yellow. Ann had one odd, multicolored marble that represented herself, and she always kept that one slightly apart from the others. A few drab, chipped ones were the school cooks. When the marbles were lined up neatly, they were in math or science class. Sometimes Ann mixed them all up violently to simulate recess . . . or one of Miss Delray's "learning experiences."

Today, however, she couldn't muster the energy or imagination for a fun game. What had happened to all the bright resolutions made that Saturday morning just a few weeks earlier? Her room was a mess, her homework was ignored, and she still had to go out to collect plants for her stupid project; and as for her promise to be nicer to Isabelle . . . How do you put something like that on THE PILE?

She stared dully at her marbles. This one is red, she thought. I see the color and I call it red. But what if . . . what if somebody else were to look at it and see the color I call blue but call that color red. How could you tell if this happened? It wouldn't help to ask them what color it was, because they would *say* red even if it *was* blue. They would have been taught to say "red" when they saw blue. Their red would *be* blue. But doesn't red have to be red? Isn't red *something?* Not just a name or label?

Ann stopped short. This is thought, she thought. This is *pure thought.*

And now I'm thinking about thought!

Has anyone else ever thought about this? Thinking about who had thought about thought made her dizzy, so Ann decided to lie down for a quick nap before getting to her science project. When she awoke, it was already dark. She plodded through dinner in silence, then borrowed her father's flashlight and a brown paper bag from the kitchen. Looking out the window, she saw that it had begun to rain hard. She wasn't surprised. Life had been going like that lately. She pulled on her mother's rubber boots because she couldn't find her own and ventured out into the night.

She had intended to collect the plants in the park, but at this hour and in this weather, that was out of the question. The back yard would have to do. She scrambled around, plucking wet leaves and thrusting them into the bag. This was harder than one might suppose. The soaked leaves ripped in her hands, and the branches were often too thick to break; when she tugged, a spray of drops fell on her head and down her collar. It was too dark to see much, and it was difficult to balance the flashlight, so she wandered from one end of the yard to the other, angrily plucking and snatching at random. On the way back to the kitchen, the flashlight grew dim, then went out. Ann stumbled in the oversized boots and fell headlong into a slimy puddle of mud.

Mother sighed heavily when she saw the condition of Ann's clothes and Father looked sadly at his broken flashlight. Ann didn't say a word.

She simply clamped her jaws shut and trudged grimly upstairs. It was one of those days.

One look at the contents of the bag the next morning proved that the night's search had been an utter waste of time. Ann drew out a handful of sticky, shapeless vegetable matter and stared at it glumly. This leaf collection project was every bit as stupid and horrid as Miss Delray's awful play was. Was Mrs. Weed getting ideas from Miss Delray in the teachers' lounge? Why? Why can't we look at a nice clean book filled with pictures of plants and learn about them that way? Ann wondered. I want school to be old-fashioned, like in books. I don't want any more "interesting projects" and "stimulating activities." I, for one, do *not* learn more by doing things myself, except that now I've learned to hate science, and that might have taken longer to find out from books. I guess that's one good thing about do-it-yourself school: you see right away what you hate!

In science class, Fernando and Lily enthusiastically showed Ann what they had done so far. Lily had made a display of what are commonly called weeds: dandelions, crabgrass, thistles, and other undesirable plants. She intended to show that they were weeds only because they were unwanted, not because of any characteristic of their own. For example, a rose would be a weed in a wheatfield. Fernando had gathered leaves from trees in the arboretum, which was clever because he hadn't had to look up the names since all the tree trunks were clearly labeled.

"And on my way back from the arboretum, guess who I met," Fernando said, laughing.

"Who?" Ann asked.

"Lily! We didn't have anything special to do, so we got the idea of going to the train station to look around."

"I go to the train station a lot," Lily said. "I like to look at everyone's face and try to guess what they're thinking. It's good training for mind reading. To be a seer you have to be born with the gift, but you also have to study human nature and learn to observe."

"She's really good at it, too, Ann," Fernando said with admiration. "We sat on a bench next to the magazine stand, and Lily told me about everyone who walked by. She said one old lady was going to visit her sick son, and a little girl was on her way to a new boarding school, and a sad-looking man had just lost his job. She seemed to know *everything*."

Ann had an impulse to ask how Fernando knew Lily's descriptions were accurate. After all, anyone with a good imagination might have said those things. She herself often watched the faces of passersby and made up stories about their lives. She also considered mentioning that she, too, might well have the Gift. But she decided it would be petty to raise doubts when they had obviously enjoyed themselves so much.

"Then, you know what?" Lily said. "Fernando helped a Spanish family who didn't speak any English to buy their tickets. And they were so grateful to find someone who spoke their language, they talked to each other for a long time."

"They had a funny accent," Fernando said. "Sort of lisping. But we could understand each other fine."

All of this sounded like great fun to Ann, and she couldn't help feeling a little left out. I wonder if they like one another better than they like me, she thought. Maybe instead of making two friends, all I did was to introduce two friends to one another, and now they don't need me anymore.

"What are you collecting for the science project, Ann?" Lily asked.

"Oh . . ." Ann said vaguely, ". . . it's a surprise."

"Ah, Ann . . . You *do* know this is due on Monday," Fernando said hesitantly.

"Of *course!*" Ann said with an edge to her voice.

"She knows, Fernando," Lily said. "She'll have it in on time. We can rely on Ann." She smiled at Ann, who smiled back weakly, feeling rather uncomfortable.

After school, Ann's mother greeted her in the

kitchen with a sandwich and a glass of milk.

"Ann," she said, "I talked to Aunt Hermina on the telephone today, and she asked if you would like to come out to the island and visit her and Uncle Alphonse at the farm this weekend."

Remembering her mother's recent scolding, Ann wondered who had really suggested this: Aunt Hermina or Mother. Aunt Hermina was an old, rather sullen woman who lived with her brother, Alphonse, on the island farm that had been in the family since before the Revolutionary War. Ann didn't see them very often because they didn't much like having visitors and they flatly refused to come in to the city. It was hard to imagine Aunt Hermina suddenly getting an overwhelming urge to see Ann.

"I don't know," Ann said suspiciously.

"It would be fun, honey," Mother said eagerly. "And I can't think of a better place for you to get plants for your project."

She's thought out all the angles, Ann thought grimly. Obviously, she won't rest until I'm out of the house. Still, Mother was right about the plants, and the farm was a pretty place, as best Ann could remember.

"All right, I'll go. Do you want me to call her back and tell her I can come?"

Mother hesitated for a moment.

"As a matter of fact, I told her this morning that you would probably be delighted to accept her invitation," she said.

A-ha! Just as little Ann had suspected. The whole thing was a plot. She was being thrown out of the house, chased away by her own mother. The bad sister was being exiled to a distant island.

Before bed, Isabelle came mournfully up to Ann's room.

"You're so lucky. Just because you're older, you get to do everything," she said. "You get to go to Aunt Hermina's farm, and I have to stay here. They have pigs and chickens and cows and everything." And she thrust out her lower lip. Even her pout was cute!

Ann had thought of this trip as something between a punishment and a chore, but now she changed her mind. If it was something Isabelle envied, it was clearly more desirable.

"I know," she said, beaming. "I can hardly wait."

"And I'm not going to have anyone to play with here. Promise you'll tell me everything you do. And how many animals there are. And what size they are. And what they eat. And what color they are. And their names."

Ann promised. She even went so far as to say that it was too bad Isabelle couldn't come along too. And she admitted that sometimes it *was* unfair to have the advantage of being the older.

Considering this, one might imagine Ann would have been pleased when, the next morning over breakfast, Mother and Father announced that they had decided to send Isabelle to Aunt Hermina's as well. Isabelle shouted for joy as she ran to pack her things.

Ann was stonily silent.

"You see," Father explained, "Isabelle would have so much fun, it seems a pity not to let her go. And your mother and I think it might be a very good idea for the two of you to be alone together in a new place. You have been quarreling a good deal recently, and a change might be just what you need. We're going to put you in charge, and I'm sure the two of you will get along beautifully."

Ann was not so sure.

It was raining lightly when the two girls and Mother reached the ferry landing.

"I'm so glad you brought raincoats," Mother said as she bought the tickets. "Do you have your money, Ann? Good. And the suitcase? Isabelle, remember to give these flowers to Aunt Hermina when you arrive. Oh, and be sure to thank her when you leave. I'll be here tomorrow at three o'clock to pick you up. Button your jacket, dear. Do you think you should have brought your boots?"

Ann stood stiffly while her mother babbled. It

would serve Mother right if everything went wrong, she thought cruelly. Ann viewed herself as the victim of a double treachery. First this trip had been foisted on her, and then, when it appeared that it might be the least little bit of fun, she had been burdened with Isabelle as a traveling companion. Anything to prevent Ann from enjoying herself!

The whistle blew, and the sisters went up the ramp onto the boat. Isabelle jumped up and down on the deck, waving good-bye to Mother, but Ann pretended to be absorbed in the workings of the ferry crew and didn't look at Mother at all.

"If it gets cold, remember to wear your long underwear!" Mother called as the ferry began to pull out from the slip. Ann stiffened with embarrassment as two old ladies smiled fondly at the girls.

"What?" Isabelle called down to her mother.

"Remember your long underwear!"

"Our long underwear?"

"Yes-s-s!" Ann hissed between her teeth, squeezing Isabelle's hand hard to make her be quiet about it.

"We will! We will!" Isabelle cried down to her mother. "We'll wear our long underwear if it gets cold!" The old ladies laughed. That was too much. Ann pulled Isabelle's hand and dragged her inside. After they had settled into two seats near

the window, Ann gazed out through the drop-
lets of sea water and tried to lose herself in a
game . . .

*And so little Ann found herself aboard a tramp steamer
on her way to live with a relative she had never seen.
Her parents had died of jungle fever only a few weeks
before, and now she was all alone in the world, obliged
to become a migrant agricultural laborer and toil from
dawn to dusk under the baking sun. Bravely, she promised herself that she would —*

"Annie," Isabelle said, "I miss Mommy."

Ann's game evaporated. Why was every game
ruined, ruined, ruined?

"You can't miss her already," she said.

"But I do!" Isabelle insisted. "I miss Mommy!"

"You just saw her ten minutes ago!" Ann nearly
screamed. How stupid could this child be? Ann
stared hard out the window and tried to recap-
ture the thread of her story . . .

*Little Ann realized that this final blow of fate would
ruin her career and her chances of being successful and
famous, but she —*

"Can I have some cocoa?" Isabelle asked.

It was no use!

"They don't have any," Ann said without looking around.

"Yes they do. I just saw a man with some."

Ann dug into her pocket and handed Isabelle
some money.

"Annie, I don't want to go alone. Come with me."

Ann snorted in martyrdom, pulled Isabelle to the refreshment stand, bought the cocoa, declined to have anything herself (although the cocoa smelled delicious), and brought the paper cup back to their seats.

"Here," she said savagely. "And don't you dare spill it."

"Thanks."

"And where are you girls going?" asked a friendly voice. It came from a middle-aged woman seated across from them.

Ann wondered why adults always assume that all children are eager to chat and why they assume that anything children are doing is a matter of public concern. She took out a book and buried herself in it without answering, hoping Isabelle would do the same. No such luck.

"We're going to Aunt Hermina's. She has pigs and cows."

"Isn't she cute?" the woman cooed to her neighbor, who leaned her face toward the girls and smiled a wide, yellow smile.

"What's your names, dearies?"

Spot and Fido, Ann thought grimly to herself.

But Isabelle introduced herself and Ann and went on to tell the ladies her father's and mother's names as well.

Be sure you tell them about our long underwear, Ann thought, staring hard at the page of
her book.

"Oh, isn't she the cutest thing?" the second
woman said.

She's cute, all right, Ann thought. Too cute for
me.

"I'm going outside," she told Isabelle. "You wait
here."

Ann stood at the bow of the boat, her hands on
the wet, cold railing, and narrowed her eyes
against the blowing spray. The boat grumbled and
vibrated as it pulled steadily out into the bay. Gulls
shrieked, and the ferry whistle blew. Ann was
alone, since the rain had discouraged the other
passengers from coming out on deck. She shivered satisfyingly. Then she was struck by a pleasant realization. Nobody knows where I am, she
thought. A few people know I'm on this boat, but
nobody knows exactly where I am on the boat or
where the boat is in the water. Boat . . . Sister Angela told me I was going to take a trip on a boat
soon, and she was right! But even she doesn't know
exactly where I am right now. Or . . . does she?
It was very hard to say. Ann gave up puzzling
over it and entered into a new story . . .

*Little Ann was a refugee. When war broke out in her
country, she was obliged to flee from the heel of oppres-
sion and seek safety in foreign lands. She would have*

to fend for herself . . . Then Ann thought of a way to include Isabelle in the story, since she was burdened with her anyway. *Little Ann had a younger sister to provide for as well as herself. She had promised her dying parents — who had always favored the cute younger sister — that she would care for her no matter what happened.* Was it bad to pretend that Mother and Father were dead? Oh, well . . . *Through thick and thin, Ann would stay by her sister's side, sometimes going without food for days so that cute little Isabelle could have her usual feasts, topped off with cocoa.*

When Ann returned to her sister's side, she was in a new and saintly frame of mind, induced by the story she had been living out in her imagination. By this time, Isabelle was entertaining half the compartment with stories about her doll, Segeener, whom she had made dance for everybody on her lap. Ann swallowed her annoyance and put her arm around her sister.

"Would you like some more cocoa?" Refugee Ann asked, *knowing full well that the cost of the cocoa would require her to go hungry for days.*

"No, thanks," Isabelle answered with a smile. *Ann protected her sister from the knowledge that they were in dire financial straits.*

"Button your sweater, dear. I wouldn't like you to catch cold," Ann said, *suppressing a shiver so her sister wouldn't know that she had no warm sweater of her own, having sold hers to pay for candy for Isabelle.*

"I'm not cold." Isabelle was surprised at the change in her sister.

"Would you like me to read to you?" Ann asked, *though she feared her fingers might be too numb to turn the pages.*

"No, thanks. I don't like your books."

How could they play refugee if Isabelle wouldn't cooperate? Ann looked at her thoughtfully and wondered what would happen if she told her about the game. She had never tried including Isabelle in her private stories before, and it might be a dangerous thing to do, but . . .

"Isabelle," she said softly, "let's pretend we're refugees on this boat, going to a new country all by ourselves because our parents were killed in the war."

Isabelle's eyes lit up. "Okay," she answered in an equally low and confidential tone. "What will our names be? Can mine be Sophia?"

Ann was delighted by how quickly Isabelle caught on, especially since she almost certainly didn't know what a refugee was. And it was a good addition to make up new names.

"Okay, Sophia," Ann said. "And mine will be Ingrid."

"Can Segeener's name still be Segeener?"

"Sure," Ann said generously. Segeener didn't sound like an American name anyway.

Ann began to narrate. "Sophia and Ingrid had

no mother and no father, and they had to go far away in a boat —"

"And Segeener too."

"All right. And Segeener too. Wait! I have a great idea. We don't speak English!"

"What do we speak?" Isabelle asked, her eyes round with excitement.

"Something like this," Ann said. "Groubles futsa dumba studda fwansoon oompanana kulker —"

"What did you say, dear?" the woman across from them asked, looking up from her magazine and smiling at Isabelle.

Isabelle looked at her flatly. "Oompanana kulker?" she asked, her eyes round with hopeful expectation.

The woman appeared confused and offended as Ann and Isabelle howled with laughter.

CHAPTER ELEVEN

Fun on the Farm

Aunt Hermina was standing on the dock when the ferry pulled in. She was a small old woman with a wrinkled face and big hands, and she dressed and walked like a man. Ann and Isabelle were used to the flowered dress, little hat, shopping bag variety of old ladies, and Aunt Hermina always seemed strange, with her dirty overalls, baggy sweater, and heavy boots. She greeted the girls gruffly and tossed their bag into the trunk of the car with surprising ease. Then she sprang into the huge rusty vehicle and the three of them drove off. Although she was so small she could barely see over the wheel, she drove very fast, occasionally muttering at passing cars that failed to get out of her way.

They went along in silence. Ann was used to answering questions from adults instead of speaking up herself, so she waited for Aunt Hermina to open the conversation. Isabelle gazed wide-eyed around the car and leaned over to whisper in Ann's ear, "There's *hay* in the back of the car."

"Sh-h-h." Ann had noticed it too, and had thought it rather strange, but she knew better than to whisper about it in front of Aunt Hermina, just as it wasn't right to point at a person with one leg.

The silence began to make Ann uncomfortable as mile after mile went by. Finally Aunt Hermina spoke.

"How's your mother?"

"Oh, she's fine," Ann answered eagerly. And then she couldn't think of anything to add. "Yes, she's fine," she repeated vaguely. "She . . . uh . . . she had a dinner party."

"What?"

"Well, it's just . . . She had a dinner party." Ann cringed. It had been a silly enough thing to say in the first place, and now it sounded incredibly stupid. Why do people always ask you to repeat the dumbest things you say? That shouldn't be allowed.

"Party, eh? Hmph."

At last Aunt Hermina pulled up the dirt drive to the side of a farmhouse with peeling white paint. Ann noticed that the front door was partially covered with vines. It must not have been used for a very long time. Aunt Hermina took the suitcase out of the car and led the girls around to the back door.

The kitchen was a large warm room with a huge fireplace and a linoleum floor, and it smelled strongly of coffee. Aunt Hermina dug through a pile of dirty dishes in the sink and finally produced two cups that were fairly clean. She filled them with coffee and set them on the table. Then she stood on a chair to reach into a high cupboard and brought down an ancient-looking bag of cookies, which she set on the table.

"Oh, uh . . . here, Aunt Hermina," Isabelle said shyly, holding out the bouquet.

"What's this?" Aunt Hermina asked, staring blankly at the flowers, and Ann felt it must seem silly to bring flowers from the city to the country. But she had had enough of being embarrassed, so she briskly rinsed out a peanut butter jar and thrust the bouquet into it, humming loudly all the while.

"There," she said. "These flowers are from Mother," she explained cheerily, setting them squarely on the table.

Aunt Hermina tucked down the corners of her mouth and looked at the flowers; then she bobbed her head, as though to say that they were certainly flowers, all right, whether or not they had any use in the house. Then she muttered something about chickens and went outside. Isabelle and Ann relaxed as soon as they were alone.

"Why doesn't she talk?" Isabelle asked.

Ann shrugged and tucked down the corners of her mouth and bobbed her head, and they both laughed into their palms.

Isabelle took a timid sip of the coffee and made a face. She tried to improve it with plenty of milk and sugar, but there was no disguising the taste.

"Why does she give us coffee?" she asked, pouring hers neatly down the sink. "Does she think we're grown up?"

"All people on farms drink coffee," Ann said importantly, gulping hers down to get it over with and trying not to shudder. She hadn't added anything to her coffee because that was the way Father drank it: black. She knew that if she was going to have an office and a job, she'd have to get used to the taste. Drinking coffee was one of the burdens of being an adult. Isabelle put a cookie in her mouth, clamped down with her teeth, then took it back out, whole and undented. The cookie was rock hard. The two girls burst into laughter.

"I guess if you work on a farm all day, you don't have much time to cook," Ann said. Clearly, all those things in books about pies cooling on windowsills were lies.

Ann and Isabelle left the remains of their snack

on the table and went to explore the rest of the house. Besides the kitchen, there were two rooms downstairs, both unheated and apparently unused. The first was a musty-smelling living room with a sofa and a few overstuffed chairs, some faded photographs of people posing stiffly, and a grandfather's clock that had stopped running. Aunt Hermina told them later that this was called the parlor and it used to be reserved for receiving the minister, for family gatherings on Christmas, and for laying out the dead, but it hadn't been used for years. Ann did not choose to pursue this matter of "laying out the dead," scarily fascinating though it was. The second room was absolutely empty, save for a large crate containing an electric stove they had received as a gift from Ann's mother and father more than ten years before. Aunt Hermina and Uncle Alphonse evidently preferred the old wood-burning stove that heated the kitchen. Like the kitchen, both of these rooms had speckled linoleum floors. Ann had never seen a living room with a linoleum floor before, and she wasn't sure she approved.

Upstairs, there were three bedrooms. The first two looked very much alike: the beds were unmade and the walls were lined with work clothes hanging on pegs. Ann put their suitcase in the third room. "Cheerful" would not be the best word to describe it, but at least the bed was made.

"I'm glad Mommy and Daddy aren't really dead and we don't really have to live here," Isabelle whispered. Ann had to agree.

"Come on, let's go outside," Isabelle suggested.

Braving the light rain to explore, the girls noticed that the outbuildings were as immaculate as the house was untidy. In the tool shed, shiny hoes, rakes, shovels, and hand tools hung in neat rows on the walls. The dirt floor was carefully swept. Ann was intrigued by this tool shed; its tidiness appealed to her thirst for order and routine. Work goes on here, she thought. You come out here early in the morning, pick up some tools, work all day, then you come back and clean the tools and hang them up on these nails. Peering more closely, Ann noticed that the heads of the nails were square. Certainly, many things were different in the country.

Next they went into the chicken coop, where the chickens cocked their heads and made low, nervous, interrogative sounds.

"Chickens!" Isabelle squealed, beside herself with excitement. She took a handful of grain from a metal trash can and squatted down, hand outstretched, hoping they would eat from it. But the hens only one-eyed her suspiciously. When she threw the grain onto the straw, the hens scrambled forward to peck.

"They're eating!" Isabelle cried. She had seen

enough books about life on a farm to recognize an eating chicken when she saw one.

The barn held even grander delights for Isabelle. There were real pigs and cows, both larger and much dirtier than they looked in books. Also, the books never mentioned the hordes of flies, which Ann found quite maddening. But Isabelle didn't seem to mind as she leaned pluckily through the wooden slats to pet the pigs.

"Should we name this one Charlie?" she asked.

Ann didn't have any opinion in the matter and the flies were becoming too much for her, so she left Isabelle cooing over the animals and went back outside. It had occurred to her that the vegetable garden might be a good place to get plant specimens for her science project. She found Aunt Hermina digging in a large patch of dirt behind the barn.

"Aunt Hermina, where is the vegetable garden?" Ann asked politely.

"What do you mean?" Aunt Hermina asked gruffly.

"Well, I . . . I just wondered where the vegetable garden is."

"This is it. Right here. Where do you think?"

Ann glanced around in confusion. The muddy patch didn't look at all like the lush, neat gardens in her books. "But . . . but where are the vegetables?"

"I'm planting. There won't be any vegetables until summer."

Ann flushed with embarrassment. Of course, vegetables were planted in the spring. How could she have forgotten?

"Oh, I know that," she stammered. "But what I meant was . . . Is there anything on the farm that's growing right now?"

Aunt Hermina stopped digging. She looked at the grass, the trees, the shrubs, then at Ann. "How do you mean?"

Ann's heart sank. She couldn't seem to stop saying stupid things. Quickly, she explained her project, and it sounded more ridiculous than ever.

"But how can sticking leaves on paper help you learn about plants?" Aunt Hermina wanted to know.

Ann confessed that she had no idea.

"Then why do you do it?"

"Because the teacher assigned the project," Ann explained.

"Why'd she do that?"

Ann refused to be put in the position of defending an assignment she herself thought was silly. "We have to do it. I don't know why."

"Well," Aunt Hermina said grudgingly after a pause, "I got all kinds of herbs inside. I guess they would do as well as anything. Particularly as the whole thing doesn't make any sense in the first place. I'll show them to you after supper."

The herb collection would be perfect! Ann thanked Aunt Hermina and set off over the fields at a fast pace, eager to avoid any more conversation in which she was sure to end up sounding stupid.

The rain had stopped, but the ground was still muddy. Ann tried to dodge the bigger puddles, but even so she soaked her shoes and muddied her pants halfway to her knees. A stone wall divided the first field from the second, and beyond that was a wood. Ann eased her way gingerly between two strands of barbed wire and entered the wood cautiously. She was almost sure there were no bears or wolves in this part of the country, but it couldn't hurt to keep an eye open. An eerie green light filtered down through the leaves, and peculiar sounds came from deeper in the wood. Ann decided to stop and sit down on a wet log. It wasn't that she was afraid to go any farther. Not really. No. She just wanted a rest.

Ann felt cold and lonely. Until three o'clock the next day seemed an awfully long time to wait before going back home. She thought of her own cozy bedroom that would be all alone that night, missing her, probably. Then something upsetting occurred to her. What if the dream came that night and she wasn't there? The sister would call and call in vain, and she would think that Ann had abandoned her. Ann tried to push the thought aside. At all events, it wasn't very likely to happen. It seemed as though the dream was gone forever. Ann sighed and started back to the house.

By the time she arrived, the others were sitting down to supper. Supper, Ann was surprised to discover, consisted of pancakes, syrup, sausage, and, of course, coffee. Uncle Alphonse smiled shyly at Ann when she sat down, but that smile was all the welcome there was. He was old and wrinkled like Aunt Hermina, and both of them had stiff, angular movements, but he moved slowly, whereas she was nimble and jerky.

"How far did you go on your walk, Annie?" Isabelle asked.

Ann calculated for a minute. "About twelve blocks," she answered.

Uncle Alphonse burst into laughter and brought his gnarled fist down on the table with startling force. "Twelve blocks!" he gasped. "That's a good 'un!"

Aunt Hermina smiled, and Isabelle laughed to see Uncle Alphonse laugh so hard that tears came to his eyes. Ann stiffened, her dignity offended. Of course she knew perfectly well that there were no blocks in the country. It was simply a way to estimate distance, and she couldn't see anything particularly funny about it. Ann was enjoying country life less and less.

"Twelve blocks!" Uncle Alphonse wheezed and collapsed into fresh gales of laughter. Ann scowled and ate steadily. Fortunately, Isabelle's cheery chatter about the animals succeeded eventually in getting his mind off those twelve blocks. Isabelle was extremely taken with Charlie, who was, it turned out, a hog, not a pig. Ann wondered grumpily what difference it could possibly make whether an animal was a hog or a pig. She longed for sidewalk cracks to step on.

After dinner Aunt Hermina showed Ann the herbs she had growing in pots on the windowsill and a shelf above. After climbing up on a rickety chair and teetering on tiptoes as she ransacked her way through top cupboards, she produced a pair of scissors, some tape, a pen, a large piece of white cardboard, and several smaller pieces of colored paper. Ann set to work snipping off the tops of the plants, taping them to the cardboard, and labeling them neatly while Aunt Hermina told her about the various herbs. Basil, thyme, parsley, anise . . . Ann wondered at first why Aunt Hermina grew these herbs. She certainly didn't use them in her cooking. Maybe it was just a farm tradition. But Aunt Hermina told her how this herb was used for stomachache, that one for headaches, and another for warding off winter flu, and there was even one that grew wild called joe-pye weed that was supposed to help mend broken bones — just how, Aunt Hermina couldn't explain. Ann wrote all the information down on squares of colored paper and taped them next to the plant. They worked together for several hours at the kitchen table, and Ann was surprised when her aunt made suggestions about placing the herbs to make the display look prettier. It seemed odd that this gruff old woman who wore men's overalls still had a sense of beauty.

"Of course, it's all a bunch of nonsense, if you ask me," Aunt Hermina muttered when they were almost finished. Then she smiled at Ann. "But if you're going to bother to do something, you might as well do it right."

When Ann had finished, she surveyed her work with pleasure. It would probably be one of the best projects in the class. Who else had an aunt who knew all about the medicinal properties of herbs?

Ann and Isabelle left their hosts sitting on either side of the big kitchen stove, listening to the radio, and went up to bed. Slipping into the icy sheets, they discovered that the bed sagged deeply in the middle. Cling to the edge as they might, there was no way to keep from rolling together. Just as Ann was drifting off into an uncomfortable sleep, she heard a burst of laughter from downstairs, and the dreary words wafted up to her: "Twelve blocks!"

Ann shook her head sadly. People who don't know much certainly make a lot of what they *do* happen to know.

When she awoke, Ann saw that Isabelle had already got up and gone. Ann dressed and went down to the kitchen. A fresh stack of eggy plates on the drainboard showed that the others had already eaten breakfast. Set at Ann's place at the table were a dirty cup, a coffeepot, and the old bag of cookies. How thoughtful. More coffee and rocks.

Ann decided to skip breakfast and went out to the barn, where Isabelle greeted her, wild-eyed, at the door.

"Oh, Annie, Annie!" she stammered. 'I'm so sorry! I'm really sorry!"

Ann was alarmed. "Sorry about what?"

Trembling with fear, Isabelle spoke quickly, sniffing back her tears. "I . . . I just brought it out here to show Charlie because it was so pretty. Then I . . . then I went to feed the chickens, and when I got back he . . . he . . . he'd eaten it!"

"Eaten it? Eaten what?"

"I'll help you make a new one. Really."

"Eaten it?" Ann stared in disbelief at what was left of her science project. Charlie had not only eaten all the plants, he'd also eaten most of the cardboard. The only good thing about this miserable weekend had just been eaten by a hog. This was too much! Ann grabbed Isabelle by the sweater and shook her.

"How could you, you stupid little idiot?"

"I just wanted to show him. I didn't think he'd — "

"Show him? Show Charlie? *Show a pig?*"

Ann shoved Isabelle with all her might. She went flying backward and hit her head on the corner of Charlie's pen. She screamed, and her head began to bleed.

Mother greeted the two silent, dismal girls at the ferry.

"Darlings," she cried, hugging them, "did you have a good time?"

Neither girl answered.

"Was Aunt Hermina nice? Isabelle, did you see the animals?"

Isabelle looked at the ground.

"What on earth's wrong, girls? Ann, did you get your project done?" Isabelle burst into tears.

"Yes, I finished my project," Ann said bitterly. "Then Isabelle ruined it!"

"Isabelle?" Mother looked confused. She took the sobbing Isabelle into her arms to console her and lowered the hood of her raincoat. Then she saw the bandage Aunt Hermina had put on her head. "What happened to you?"

Ann took a deep breath. This was it. Her parents would never forgive her for this one.

It was difficult for Isabelle to talk through her sobs. "I . . . I fell down."

"Oh, I'm so sorry, honey. That's bad luck. But it was naughty of you to ruin Ann's work. Ann, darling, maybe we can make a new one before tomorrow."

Ann stared at her sister. She couldn't believe it. Isabelle hadn't told on her. Isabelle *hadn't told!*

CHAPTER TWELVE

Dream Sister

Just as science class was about to begin, Ann walked up to Mrs. Weed's desk and stood there until the teacher glanced up from her work.

"Yes, Ann?" Mrs. Weed smiled at her.

"Mrs. Weed, I haven't done my project."

"What?" Mrs. Weed asked, assuming she had misunderstood.

"Lily and Fernando have done theirs, so please grade them as a regular group of two. Don't take off their grade because of me."

Mrs. Weed frowned. The class grew interested in what was happening at the teacher's desk, and a hush fell over the room.

"You haven't done your work?" Mrs. Weed asked, her words ringing out clearly in the silence.

"No."

"Do you have an excuse? An explanation?"

"No."

"Do you need more time to finish? If you'd like, you could present yours tomorrow."

"No, I'm not going to do it." Ann stared steadily at the teacher, her eyes stinging with tears that wanted to come. She felt as though she were in a bad dream. Her words caused an excited murmur in the classroom, and Ann felt her face grow hot and her ears begin to ring.

Mrs. Weed appeared bewildered. She said carefully, "You know that I'll have to give you an F, don't you, Ann?"

"I know." Ann returned to her desk and sat down.

"Well, I guess Ann isn't such a perfect student after all," Patty said triumphantly. "*Our* group is ready," she said in a loud voice. "May we go first, Mrs. Weed?"

"Yes, Patty," the teacher answered. "Quiet please, children. We are going to hear from Patty and Suzy."

During their presentation, Lily leaned over and whispered to Ann, "You should have told me. I would have said that we'd done mine together."

"No," Ann answered. "That wouldn't be fair. Anyway, it doesn't matter."

Mrs. Weed frowned sternly in their direction. "No talking, please!"

One after the other, each group gave its oral report. Ann stared down at her desk and didn't hear a word. This was the first time she had failed at anything in school, and it felt terrible. Fernando and Lily laughed and joked easily through their presentation and helped each other to answer the questions from the class. Ann felt very small and removed. After school she tried to sneak home unnoticed, but Lily and Fernando caught her at the edge of the playground.

"Ann," Lily said, "we were just saying what a waste of time that science thing was, and how right you were not to do it."

"It was good how you told Mrs. Weed right out like that," Fernando added. "Most people wouldn't have dared."

"Oh . . . well . . ." Ann said, looking the other way.

"I bet Mrs. Weed won't give us another assignment like that one. I know she cares what you think."

That made it worse. With panic, Ann realized that she was about to cry.

"Look, Ann," Lily said, "we were thinking of going back to the train station on Saturday. Do you want to come? Fernando can stop by your house, then you two can pick me up on the way. Okay?"

"Oh, I don't care," Ann answered, concentrating hard on not letting her eyes fill up with tears.

"What?"

"All right. I'll come. I have to go home now. Good-bye," Ann said very quickly and turned away just in time. They don't really want me to go with them, she thought. They just feel sorry for the stupid girl who flunked science.

That evening Ann sat on the floor of her room and tucked her knees up under her chin. Her mind was so heavy with unhappiness that even her thoughts came slowly. She had failed in school. Mrs. Weed didn't like her anymore. She had let down her only friends. Her father was angry about his broken flashlight. She had hurt Isabelle. She was a terrible sister and a terrible daughter.

She looked up and saw Pecony Bear sitting on her desk. Poor little Pecony, she thought. I've neglected him too. She took him down and cuddled him in her arms. Then she decided to dress him in an old doll's nightgown that she found at the bottom of her wardrobe, next to . . . THE PILE.

After she had slipped the nightgown on him, she tucked Pecony into her bed and crawled in alongside, leaving him plenty of room so he wouldn't get squashed during the night. Pulling the covers up to his neck carefully, she promised herself she would spend more time with him from now on.

"Don't you recognize me? Even now?"

The voice was distant and barely audible. Ann

dreamt she sat upright in bed. She had almost forgotten about the dream in the torrent of misfortunes that had befallen her lately. Of course! The dream! It was the only thing she had left now. She ran to the window and looked out over the carnival lights.

"This time . . ." she told herself, "this time I don't want to come back. I want to stay in the dream forever and ever. Don't make me come back. Please, please, don't make me."

The wind snatched her up, rushed her through the window, and dropped her roughly onto the ground. The carnival was hot and deafening. The air seemed filled with a dense mist, and she could make out only a blur of faces and colored lights. She staggered through the crowd, searching desperately for the Gypsy sister. I have to stay here, Ann though in a panic. I can't ever go home.

A large man loomed up out of the fog and grabbed Ann by the arm.

"Want to play, girlie-girl? A quarter for three tries. You can be a winner!"

"Let me go! I don't want to be a winner!" Ann cried, struggling to escape his grasp.

"Whaddaya saying, kid? You *got* to be a winner!"

Ann wrenched herself free and ran as fast as she could. The Gypsy's voice seemed to call to her from all directions, and she ran first this way, then that, forcing herself through the throng of faceless people, but she could find the lost sister nowhere. She ran blindly, whimpering with frustration, and suddenly . . .

She was on the top of a hill, all alone. She gasped when she saw what lay before her. The carnival stretched on endlessly . . . endless rides and booths and lights and noise and confusion flowing out to the black horizon.

"Oh, please," she cried. "Please!" A knot was forming in her chest. Ann had never wanted anything as badly as she wanted to find that little Gypsy. She needed her lost sister desperately.

Suddenly Ann was back in the din and crush of the carnival again, the crowd pressing all around her. There, at the edge of the throng, was the Gypsy, her back to Ann. Terrified that the girl might disappear again, Ann struggled through the crowd until she was close enough to grasp the girl's thin shoulders through her smooth silk scarf. With all her strength, she forced the girl to turn around until her face was in the light.

"Ann," the girl stammered, looking frightened. "Don't you recognize your own sister?"

"Yes." Ann could hardly speak. "Yes, I do! I do!" She burst into tears. It was Isabelle.

Ann awoke in tears and groped her way down the dark staircase into her sister's room. Isabelle was curled up in a little ball, sound asleep. Ann looked down at her. Of course the dream sister had been Isabelle. Not an enchantment, not Lily, not a dead sister, but Ann's real little sister. Sister Angela had said that perhaps the dreams were Ann's own attempt to tell herself something. They'd been Ann's way of telling herself that Isabelle deserved her recognition and affection. Ann slipped into the bed, put her arm around Isabelle, and hugged her.

"Annie?" Isabelle said groggily.

"Isabelle, I'm sorry I've been mean to you. I don't mean to be. It's just . . ."

"You're not mean to me, Annie," Isabelle muttered sleepily.

Ann thought of all the times she had frightened and teased Isabelle. She remembered the wolves in the closet, the silk dresser scarf, the cookies, dragging Isabelle home from the park, pushing her down in the barn . . . She ached with remorse.

"I really do love you, Isabelle, and I'm going to be good to you from now on."

Isabelle hummed contentedly as she slipped back into sleep. Ann looked at her calm face and realized that she really *did* love Isabelle. It was a strange and delightful feeling. She had always known that one was supposed to love one's family, and she had assumed that the vague blend of

understanding and envy and comfort and irritation she had felt toward Isabelle was what people
meant by love. But now, as she looked down at
her, she felt an ache in her chest and a sort of
melting feeling that she knew was real love. She
pulled Isabelle's covers up a bit and smiled at her
in the dark. Isabelle. Her sister. How lucky she
was to have a sister . . .

Ann found a new, deliciously cool spot on the
pillow for her cheek, and then slowly, bit by bit,
a wonderful idea occurred to her. I am one little
girl, she thought. I am one little girl in one room
in one house. In one house on one block of one
street in one city. In one city in one country on
one planet. In outer space there are millions and
millions of little lights, and Earth is only one of
them. I am one tiny speck on one of those tiny
lights. If that's all I am, my problems must really
be *very* small.

One by one, the things that had been worrying
her so much a few hours before drifted back into
her mind. That science project . . . How could one
little assignment on one small day in one speck of
a school on one tiny point of light in the universe
matter? Ann laughed aloud. I'm smart enough,
she thought. I won't fail in school, and Mrs. Weed
will still like me. And so will Lily and Fernando.
How could they possibly change their minds about
me because of a piece of homework? It's ridicu-

lous. And does it matter that they like being with one another? They like being with me too, don't they? Maybe she would have them both over one day soon, and the four of them (Isabelle, too) would play something together. Maybe she would even show them THE PILE.

That PILE . . . Ann laughed sleepily. I'm only ten years old, she thought, and suddenly she felt free. When I grow up, I'll do something, and whatever it is, it will be good enough. I don't have to do it now. Isabelle is right. She plays and has fun all day because she knows she's a child. I've been making myself miserable trying to be an adult and that's all wrong. I don't have to do anything now except . . . except do my schoolwork the best I can and play games and be nice to Isabelle. And give Father his hammer back. And all of that is easy. It's all very, very easy and I don't have to do anything else.

Ann stretched out and began to fall asleep.

I'm just a little girl, she thought. I'm just a little girl.